Gregson, Lee F.

Braid

SPECIAL MESSAGE TO READERS

This book is published under the auspices of

THE ULVERSCROFT FOUNDATION

(registered charity No. 264873 UK)

Established in 1972 to provide funds for research, diagnosis and treatment of eye diseases. Examples of contributions made are: —

A new Children's Assessment Unit at Moorfield's Hospital, London.

•

Twin operating theatres at the Western Ophthalmic Hospital, London.

•

A Chair of Ophthalmology at the University of Leicester.

•

The establishment of a Royal Australian College of Ophthalmologists "Fellowship".

You can help further the work of the Foundation by making a donation or leaving a legacy. Every contribution, no matter how small, is received with gratitude. Please write for details to:

THE ULVERSCROFT FOUNDATION,
The Green, Bradgate Road, Anstey,
Leicester LE7 7FU, England.
Telephone: (0116) 236 4325

In Australia write to:
THE ULVERSCROFT FOUNDATION,
c/o The Royal Australian College of Ophthalmologists,
27, Commonwealth Street, Sydney,
N.S.W. 2010.

BRAID

Heading for Coldheart, on the sniff of a peacekeeping job, Braid found an unlikely companion in Rachel, one of a farm family travelling by wagon. In the violent town, Braid struck a bargain, but he recognized that the girl's presence was unwelcome. However, as he set about bringing law to the lawless streets, the resentments were allowed to simmer. Then came the attempt on the bank, and when the smoke of the fierce gun-battle had cleared, Braid and his girl faced one final challenge.

Books by Lee F. Gregson
in the Linford Western Library:

THE MAN OUT THERE
THE STOREKEEPER OF SLEEMAN
LONG AGO IN SERAFINA
SEASON OF DEATH

LEE F. GREGSON

BRAID

Complete and Unabridged

LINFORD
Leicester

First published in Great Britain in 1993 by
Robert Hale Limited
London

First Linford Edition
published 1996
by arrangement with
Robert Hale Limited
London

British Library CIP Data

Gregson, Lee F.
Braid.—Large print ed.—
Linford western library
I. Title II. Series
823.914 [F]

ISBN 0–7089–7818–5

Published by
F. A. Thorpe (Publishing) Ltd.
Anstey, Leicestershire

Set by Words & Graphics Ltd
Anstey, Leicestershire
Printed and bound in Great Britain by
T. J. Press (Padstow) Ltd., Padstow, Cornwall

This book is printed on acid-free paper

1

OLVIE was as close as a long spit to the far side of the ford, in steady rain, when the left rear wheel of the wagon sank in and the heavily-laden rig slewed and stopped, the pair of horses straining and thrashing the water, Olvie up on the tilting seat knowing it was no longer any use laying the whip on; he would have to climb down and see what else could be done.

Braid, having already carried the others one by one, doubled up on the black, across the ford of the Pinder River, now dismounted, and without being asked, Rachel came to him and took hold of the mount and led it away up onto fairer ground. Olvie's wife, Bree, went sloshing down to stand between the wagging heads of the horses, grasping their bridles, her own head ducked down inside her rain-sodden hood.

Braid and Olvie thereupon set to, lashed by the rain, halfway to their knees in swirling, discoloured water, seizing hold of wheel-spokes, the big wagon seemed to hang menacingly over them.

"Now!" Braid shouted, and in unison they gave a heave and managed to get the wheel a quarter of a turn before sheer weight defeated them and the wagon rocked dangerously down again.

Chests heaving, Braid and Olvie straightened up, water streaming from the brims of their hats, slickers gleaming, and made gestures which amounted to an agreement that for their next attempt they must seize hold of spokes lower down. Braid signalled by nodding, and again they bent their backs.

"Ready?"

"Yep!"

"Now!"

To their straining tendons up it came

ever so slowly, and to the woman calling and tugging at the horses, her feet slipping sometimes, all under the unceasing oppression of the rain.

"Hea-ve!"

All at once it was free and crawling up onto firmer footing, Braid and Olvie still bending at the wheel-spokes, until the team was being walked forward easily by the woman and brought to a halt.

Crouching ineffectually under dripping brush the three younger Olvie children called and even waved during the slow, straining triumph of mother and father and the big man, Braid. Now, bent over, they ran to get in under the shelter of the wagon-bed, Gage who was six years old, Aaron who was eight and May, a girl of thirteen. The eldest, Rachel, in budding womanhood, now led Braid's black horse forward and hitched it to the tailgate of the wagon.

Braid and Olvie, Olvie's wife and this girl, Rachel, came slopping around to stand in what was more or less the lee of the vehicle, a wagon festooned with casks and cannisters, and in the steady noise of the rain began talking about what the next move ought to be. Rachel did not take much part in the discussion, hunched in a hooded cloak that was heavily wet, but stood watching Braid and paying attention, in the main, to what he said.

Some hundred yards beyond where they were now, through sparse brush, they could glimpse what appeared to be a clear area large enough for a camp, though while the rain continued there would be no possibility of getting a fire going.

Braid then indicated the ravaged, moving sky, and though the downpour seemed to belie it, he offered an opinion that the rain might soon ease; and he pointed towards uneven, higher ground beyond the clearing and some outcrops of rock.

"Could be some dry brush down in among those," he said, and Olvie nodded and together they headed off to find out if it might be so. After they had gone a dozen paces Braid glanced back and saw, as he had expected, that Rachel was coming too.

They had travelled together for several weeks, Braid glad enough of the company, the Olvies of the presence of the quiet, hard man whom they felt instinctively could be trusted, going across an expanse of less-than-friendly territory. From the beginning he had fitted in, fetched his own supplies and had been respectful of all the females; but here at the Finder River was where they knew they would part, the Olvies following the course of the Pinder, more or less north-east, Braid riding westward. Olvie and Braid had talked about it once, over an evening fire.

"When yuh get there, what line o' work will it be?"

"Peacekeeping."

"What town is it?"

"Coldheart."

"Mebbe when yuh do get there,

yuh'll find the work ain't kept this long."

"We'll see. When word came to me it took its own good time, so the work still being there or not is a chance I have to take. When I get there I've got to see a man named Bessemer."

The Olvies were not in good shape. Food was no longer in plentiful supply and Braid had observed that the woman, for one, was eating less, so too was Rachel, making sure that the children were kept fed. And it was not as though the family was travelling with any kind of plan in mind; there was more hope involved in it than much else, and less of that as the days wore on and the weather continued bad.

On occasions Braid still took time to stare back the way they had come and also examined the surrounding country, or as much of it as was to be seen in such poor visibility. During the past week they had come by chance upon others on the move and a couple of them, at least, had not been much to Braid's liking, a pair of ragged saddle-tramps, one wearing a pair of patched and stained Confederate cavalry pants, unclean men with bad teeth and worse breath, who had eyed all of the Olvie females and had shown a certain reluctance to leave.

As far as Olvie himself was concerned, it was simply one more thing that had to be worried about along with the damned wet and the cold and the fact that the scarcity of food for his family was a worsening problem. The presence of Braid, however, had in no way contributed to that. Braid carried his own provisions and indeed had shown a propensity to share what little he had. The plain fact was that they were coming under increasing pressure on a journey full of uncertainties.

Among the rocky outcrops, though having to work their way around with care, they did discover some relatively thornless brush which, if covered and kept under the wagon, would be still dry enough to light as soon as the rain eased off. Each of them carried an armful back to the camp-site and stacked it beneath the wagon and Olvie fetched from inside the wagon a spare piece of canvas which they weighted around the edge with stones and spread over the brush.

The thirteen-year-old, May, and the two Olvie boys, Gage and Aaron, established themselves in the lee of this covered brush and prepared to wait with the uncomplaining patience that Braid had observed in all the Olvies, until conditions should improve. The mother, Bree, went there too, hunkering down with her younger children, while Olvie, assisted by Braid, unharnessed the wagon team and led the two horses across the clearing, and with light cords tethered them to picket pins. Rachel, as she now often did, worked quietly alongside Braid, the mother's eyes following both of them as they went doggedly about numerous tasks.

In something less than an hour and as Braid had predicted, the rain stopped, the sky now moving with torn leaden clouds, and though the wind dropped too, it was still cold and uncomfortable. Rachel gathered some smooth stones and set about arranging the place for the fire, then Olvie summoned his three younger children and headed off with them to fetch more brush to be stockpiled for the night. Bree Olvie climbed up into the wagon to sort out what food was to be cooked for supper. When Olvie came back he tipped out some feed for all of the animals.

When coffee was ready Rachel poured a tin cupful for Braid and fetched it to him, handing it over with great care and the flicker of a smile.

"Supper won't be long."

He studied her as she went about her work, helping her mother, checking and guiding the younger brood. May, he noticed, tended to imitate her, perhaps seeing virtue in emulating her; but May, at thirteen, was gangly and inclined to clumsiness so that

Rachel often needed to speak to her quietly and show her again. Rachel, it seemed to him, was as capable as Bree herself. Occasionally Rachel glanced up and caught him looking at her, regarding him in return with her large, dark eyes.

Later, at the fire, huddled against the cold, Olvie said to him: "Tomorrow then, to Coldheart."

Braid nodded. "And you, for Blayrock."

Rachel, sitting near Braid, stared into the fire.

Later still Braid, irritatingly troubled about the men who had fallen in with them on the previous day, and having deliberately left the black saddled, retightened cinches, mounted up and rode off into the deep gloom towards the ford of the Finder. He was away for maybe half an hour and when he returned to the camp and unsaddled, carrying the saddle near to the fire to use as a pillow, Olvie looked up from feeding more brush onto the blaze, while sparks went leaping.

"Anything?"

"No," said Braid, "but that might not mean much." The younger ones had been bedded down in the wagon but Rachel had waited for Braid to come back. She said: "Do you think they'll come here?"

"I don't know," said Braid. "They could be miles away, still going away." He looked out at the damp dark that surrounded them all and shrugged. "I don't know." When he fetched his bedroll and laid it out they saw that he had also brought his Winchester carbine and he slid it in under the saddle out of sight.

Bree Olvie climbed up into the wagon to sleep with her children, Braid, Olvie and Rachel getting as near to the fire as they dared; and if it rained again they would crawl in under the wagon. They huddled close, Rachel in the middle. Braid took off his fleece-lined, calfskin jacket and insisted that she put it on, and wrapped himself in an extra blanket and his slicker. In spite of the cold, the exertions of the day now prevailed and they fell into a deep sleep.

2

IN the near-dark dawn they came without warning, their horses making the water of the ford fly like shattered glass, one man letting rip a mighty Rebel yell as he rode, the morning suddenly filled with the snorting and blowing and thunder of horses and of men shouting and the sight of breath streaming from humans and animals alike.

At the camp, up for an early start, all were now rising from the fire and scattering, Braid shouting "Get to the brush! Get into cover!" but Braid himself, down on one knee, was reaching cold fingers under his saddle for his 45–75 carbine and by the time the riders were weaving through the sparse brush towards the wagon under the blue haze of woodsmoke, Braid had levered a round into the chamber. Olvie had not gone running with his family but was a dozen feet to Braid's right, on his knees, crouching, watching the wild riders coming on, heading directly towards the fire, one continuing his insane yelling, both quirting the horses, counting on the stiffness of limbs in the chill air, the half-awareness of early wakefulness, and fear engendered by sudden noise and confusion.

Braid had the long stock of the carbine with its forged iron butt-plate to his shoulder, a fearsome weapon in the hands of a man like Braid, twenty-two inches of barrel, nine-round, tube magazine beneath it, each cartridge loaded with seventy-five grains of black powder and a three hundred and fifty grain lead bullet, and with a striking energy of fourteen hundred foot-pounds.

When the nearer of the two oncoming horsemen was within forty feet of him, Braid coolly shot him, the heavy bang of the carbine loud in the morning air, and the rider was punched savagely backward, hanging there a moment, then falling out of the saddle, the wild-eyed horse charging on through the camp, tin pans clanging and flying, the unhorsed man striking the cold earth with a loose, sodden noise, rolling wildly with the inertia of his approach, in spite of the bullet-strike, sliding through the hot stones and embers of the fire in a shower of sparks.

The instant the carbine went off, the second rider had veered away, angling to his right, heading for the brush beyond the camp, while Braid, having levered in a fresh round, tracked him, swinging the line of the carbine a touch ahead of the crouching, hard-riding man; then the carbine banged again, fumes wafting back, and the target was thumped sideways and went down off the horse, though one boot failed to come free at once so that the man went bouncing jerkily along until his eventual passage through thorny brush raked him violently down.

Because this one could no longer be seen clearly, Braid, his boots sliding on the wet ground as he tried to go quickly, jogged towards the place where the rider had seemed to become detached from the horse. The light was still very poor but when he came upon him he saw that some of the upper clothing had been shorn away leaving him slashed and bloodied, his body steaming in the cold air; but this man, head-shot, was now beyond all heat or chill or pain.

Braid turned and peered through the gloom, then began to go back across the clearing and he could see that Ben Olvie had gone to the first man brought down and was looking at him carefully. When Braid got nearer to him Olvie glanced up and said: "This one's yelled his last yell."

One by one the others were standing up out of hiding. Olvie had stood too, but now bent and picked up a crushed metal pot, looked at it, then dropped it again. Rachel came over in a cold, huddled way to stand near Braid. From the time they had first heard the riders splashing through the ford until this moment near the smouldering body, perhaps two and a half minutes had elapsed. All of the group now gradually came together and Olvie said:

"Might as well fetch their mounts in."

When, after fifteen minutes or so, all of them having gone out, they caught the riderless and now standing horses, Aaron the elder boy and the girl, May, led them nodding into the camp.

"Hitch 'em over there with ours," Olvie instructed, "we'll give 'em a good once-over later."

When they did take a careful look they found both animals sound enough and they could discern faded brands on the flanks, one which was simply a number 6, the other what looked like a C or maybe, as Rachel said, a half moon.

"Whatever it is," Braid observed, "both of 'em are likely stolen, but where or who from and how long ago is anybody's guess."

The clothing of the dead man who had come rolling through the fire, shot in the upper chest, was not only still smoking but in parts was aglow, and Olvie, going through the pockets, at one point hissed sharply and sucked at a finger.

"This one'll be well primed fer Old Nick by the time he gets there."

Nothing that Olvie found could identify this man who was reddish-haired and who wore over a black shirt a filthy wet-weather coat that reached to around his knees, grey cavalry pants and very scuffed boots, one with an old gash in the side, a wide leather belt, a shellbelt with only four rounds remaining in it, an old fashioned pistol, loaded in three of its chambers; and the hat that had gone lifting away when he came down was battered and greasy. Olvie found a part-sack of Bull Durham and two dollar bills and twenty-five cents in coins. "That's it," he said, "he was travellin' real light." Then: "I'll never know why they rushed us the way they did, all the racket."

"Yesterday, maybe they didn't notice the carbine."

When they went to the body of the other one who had been hit just forward of his left ear so that his head was in something of a mess, again they were able to discover no identifying mark or paper. There was a slightly latcr-model pistol, little more ammunition than thcy had found on the first man and only seventy-three cents in coins.

The money found on both bodies, Braid insisted Olvie take. Braid also removed the shellbelts, holsters and pistols and suggested that Olvie take these as well and at the next town endeavour to sell them.

"They'll not fetch a lot," Braid said, "but anything's better than a boot in the ass in the rain."

"We'll have to set to an' bury these

bastards," said Olvie, "an' it better be deep, no matter who they was. I seen folks that's been planted too shallow an' been dug up by animals, after, or had water wash away the earth. Seen a skull stickin' right out o' the ground, once." May, edging closer, her white, pinched face serious, then asked why Braid had had to shoot them. "Why girl?" Olvie said, though not unkindly. "Because if he hadn't done it, right off, by now him an' me an' both your brothers woulda been dead there on the ground, an' you an' Rachel an' your ma woulda been wishin' you was, that's why."

"Come on May," said Bree Olvie, "come help me gather up our stuff." The girl went shuffling off after her mother.

By the time they had got the burying done the grey morning was well advanced, and though there was no further rain, a cold, tugging wind had come up again. Braid and Olvie discussed their present situation, knowing that the time to go separate ways had arrived, and both hunkered down while Braid scratched the damp earth with a stick, Rachel squatting alongside him.

"This," said Braid, drawing a line, "is the Pinder, and we're about here. If you follow the river north two days, maybe a bit less, you'll get to Blayrock. Whatever trading you want to do can be done there. Maybe there'll be work in Blayrock." Olvie rubbed at his reddened nose but offered no comment. As Braid had become well aware, he had long ago ceased to consider Providence seriously. "Beyond Blayrock, if you're still following this river," Braid said, "is Margarita."

"And you, you go west from here," said Olvie.

Braid made other marks with the stick.

"Yeah. About here, about a day's ride beyond that broken country over there (waving a hand vaguely to his left) the word I have is that there's a trader, Keast, runs a way station as well, for east-west stages. I've got a few bills left, not many, but I can get me more supplies there, enough to take me up across the high country beyond there, to Coldheart."

Olvie nodded, sniffed, rubbed at his nose.

"This place, this Coldheart," he said, "yuh say it's a mine?"

"No, there's gold claims though, up along the Poison River, going up among high canyons, but all across the Coldheart Plateau there's cattle. Anyway, that was what I had from the man I've got to see there, Bessemer."

Olvie studied the marks on the ground as though he might have been examining ancient runes, then looked up at Braid.

"There's somethin' to talk out between us now."

Rachel glanced at her father, then at Braid, then away. Braid nodded almost imperceptibly, his limbs cold and stiffening, but he remained hunkered there with Olvie and Rachel. She had listened keenly to all that had been said but had remained silent. She had on her old grey cape with the hood up, her smooth, delicate face and large, very dark eyes making her resemble some small, wary animal staring out of its burrow. A strand of hair was trembling across her brow. Olvie made a sign and Bree Olvie, perhaps watching for it, told her other children to climb up into the wagon some little distance away, to be ready to move, then Bree herself came across and stood behind her husband, the wind tugging at her shabby skirts. When she had been moving and now, as she stood calmly waiting, it was clear to Braid, and not for the first time, where Rachel had got her looks and her way of moving.

Unremarked until now, for it was plain that Olvie was to bring it into the open, there had grown between Braid and Rachel a quiet alliance. It was something that had come about subtly and naturally, in the way that some people and some creatures are drawn into an affinity, though it had been a development less of Braid's initiative than of hers; yet there had been no hint of archness, no ridiculous mating dance. As day had followed day on this uncomfortable journey she had simply chosen to sit with him, to pour his coffee, to prepare his food. Once, the younger girl, May, had said something to her that had caused a quick, minor flare-up between them, and when Bree Olvie had called out to them, wanting to know what it was about, May had reddened and dropped her eyes and Rachel had said: '*It was nothing*' and Bree had chosen to let it go at that. Now Braid knew that what was to be discussed was the culmination of all this in the light of the Olvies' present situation.

Olvie was no fool and neither was his worn, tired little wife. Life had fashioned them into realists, pragmatists. Things were as they were, often beyond the powers of individual men and women to alter them. Each day must be got through the best way possible. Regrets over what might have been were pointless. There was no room for self-indulgence, certainly not for self-pity. And the reality was that the Olvies were moving ever so slowly with diminishing resources into a future even more uncertain than usual, with too many mouths to feed. So Olvie, the realist, now looked at his eldest child and raised his thick dark eyebrows.

"Well then Rache, is this to be it, girl?"

"You'd best ask Braid that, pa."

"Now then Rache, I'm askin' you."

"Yes."

"Braid?"

"If Rachel's of a mind," Braid turned his head slightly so that he could see her face, uncomfortable that the discussion was proceeding in this way, as though she was almost some object to be bargained over, "then I've a mind for her to come."

"They might have somethin to say about it in — where is it? — Coldheart."

"Then they'll have to say it to me."

Bree Olvie came around and across to Rachel and pulled the hood back slightly and put a hand on the girl's dark brown hair.

"Are you sure, little love?"

"I am ma. I'm sure."

Bree Olvie looked down at Braid. "Then there's no more to be said."

Olvie looked up, then down again.

Grunting from the stiffness in his knees Braid stood up, and Rachel stood too. Olvie remained squatting for a few seconds longer, looking at the marks on the ground, then he too stood up. Now there were the practicalities to be dealt with; how she would travel, what she would wear, what she would take with her.

She fancied the horse that she called Half Moon; and from the other animal she took two capacious saddlebags with a few items of filthy clothing in them and not much else. She declined both of the bedrolls that had belonged to the dead men, and nobody blamed her, seeing the state of them. The clothing and the bedrolls she burned on what was left of the camp-fire, reviving it to a stench-laden pillar of smoke. Bree agreed that as much clothing as Rachel owned that was also fit to take with her, could be got into the saddlebags.

"If you're gonna ride that horse," Olvie said to his daughter, "yuh cain't do it in what you're wearin' now."

"She can come with me," said Bree. They went to the wagon and climbed up into it, the younger Olvies being for the moment shooed away, the youngest one not yet understanding what this activity was all about.

When, less than a half-hour later, the girl emerged, she was wearing a pair of cut-down levis that must have been Olvie's, somewhat generous around the middle, for though Olvie himself was a raky individual, Rachel was wand-slim, with a very small waist. She had on too, a pair of women's lace-up boots, the cut bottoms of the levis pulled down over the tops of them, a thick blue and white checkered shirt that was large enough to wrap half around her again, her grey cloak over that, a brown felt hat with a widish brim, a red and white feather poked through one side.

While Rachel was occupied in packing the saddlebags, then slinging them up over the horse she was to ride, Bree Olvie, passing, said softly to Braid: "She's a real good girl, mister. You'll take care of her an' not strike her an' see to her churchin' when you can?"

"Just as soon as may be," Braid answered, "and I'll see to it that no harm comes to her."

Braid then made himself busy with last-minute tasks, some of which were manifestly superfluous, rechecking cinches, ensuring canteens had been filled, seeing to the securing of the bedroll on his own horse and to the large saddlebags that Rachel had slung up on Half Moon.

The Olvies were now standing all together near their wagon, the mother bleak but dry-eyed, May, clinging fast to Rachel, in tears, and the elder of the boys, like his father, with his head down. Only the younger boy seemed not to have grasped what was happening and when Rachel pulled herself away and came walking across to Braid at the horses, called: "See yuh tomorrow, Rache!"

Braid and Rachel, breath vapouring, faces cold, met briefly with their eyes. He would have helped her to mount up but she said: "I can do it," and after a couple of hopping attempts because the horse moved, did swing up and settled herself in the worn, shiny saddle.

Walking the horses from the wet camp Braid raised one gloved hand to the Olvies, then glanced up at the sky, thinking that more rain was not far away; but Rachel slap-slapped her heels a couple of times, causing the horse to go loping away. She did not look back.

3

THE westbound stage had not long departed and two surly-eyed employees had led the tired, steaming horses, the old team from the changeover, into one of the barns to be cooled and fed and watered, made ready to be the new change-team for the next stage through, nearly two days from now.

Keast's Trading Post and Way Station, this was, that had the aspect of a small, ramshackle town which for some unfathomable reason had failed to develop. There was a very large building which was the trading post itself, a couple of pole corrals, two barns and three clapboard shacks, each with an old, rusting tin chimney sticking up, like the two that protruded from the trading post and from which wisps of blue smoke curled into the overcast sky. Behind the principal building was an untidy yard, a mess of boxes and casks, an old tin tub with a rusted hole in it, some lengths of grey lumber and a miscellany of coloured bottles and discarded pots and pans. A pair of discoloured longjohns hung limply on a cord outside the back door.

The man himself, Keast, was broad and fat with a greasy, grimy skin, whose paunch was sufficient to incline his brass belt-buckle downward. His shirt was a dirty grey, with half-moons of sweat under the armpits, and he had on stained cord trousers; and now he leaned near to one of his grimy windows to watch the two riders approaching, one of them a big fellow on a fine-looking black, the other much smaller, a boy he thought, on a less-well-kept chestnut.

When they got closer he could see that the big man was clad in very faded levis and a light brown, calf-skin coat that reached to his thighs and with a turned-up collar where a fleece-lining could be seen; and he had on a wide-brimmed, discoloured black hat with a shallow crown and hanging leather thongs. His companion, recognizable now as a girl in spite of her rough, partly-male clothing, wore old levis, bulky at the middle, what seemed to be a man's blue and white checkered shirt of a thick woollen material and a grey cloak with a fallen-back hood. On her head was a rounded-crown, broad-brimmed hat of some smooth material, with a small red and white feather in it.

These two drew rein at the old hitching rail out in front of the trading post. The girl must have noticed a ghost of movement at the filthy window, then perceived the fat man looking out, and for a moment sat regarding him with large, very dark eyes.

To begin with, only the man came in, the girl not even dismounting. Braid's nose twitched when he got inside, because of the strange amalgam of smells. Keast stood regarding him warily out of small, bright, pouched eyes, and what he saw was a powerful, leather-skinned man with a once-broken nose and slate-coloured eyes, the bottom of a greasy old holster visible below the hang of his fleece-lined coat. He had dark stubble around his mouth.

When Braid perceived the variety of goods stacked and hung in jumbly rows down the dimly-lamplit store, rows that vanished into shadows, he went out again to speak to the girl.

"Best you come in an' have a look around. The place stinks an' so does the fat man if you get too close."

"So do I, most likely," she said, but swung down, slightly, uncharacteristically stiff as she stood a moment hitching the chestnut. So they trooped in.

A half-hour later, Braid making careful calculations all the while, Rachel waiting for his nod, they bought a passable bedroll for her, a pair of levis and a denim shirt that looked as though they had been made for a boy and that Rachel held against herself critically, appearing satisfied; a couple of well-made, colourful Indian blankets and a short, fleece-lined coat not unlike Braid's, but which again, because the girl was not big, came well down her thighs when she tried it on. To do this she had removed her cloak and though the man's shirt she was wearing was too large for her, the eyes of the fat man lingered on her every movement, and only when he saw Braid looking at him did he look away. Finally, though it went against the grain, Braid said:

"We've come some distance an' we've still got a good piece to go. Any place we can bed down tonight, maybe get a meal?"

Keast regarded him neutrally. Yes, but it would be extra. They could use one of the shacks, the farthest away of the three that stood behind the trading post, and he had bacon and beans and coffee that could be bought. Braid nodded, knowing that in any case he would have to replenish his supplies.

"The mounts," said Keast, "can go in the barn behind where yuh'll be. There's feed an' there's water." Naturally, all that would be extra.

When the horses had been installed in the barn, unsaddled, rubbed down and given feed, Braid and Rachel, making several trips, humped all of their belongings to the end one of all the unappealing shacks. If the two men who had attended to the stage horses were watching them, then they were covert in doing it, for though Braid glanced around numerous times he saw no-one.

The pot-bellied stove inside the shack contained remnants of tinder-dry wood in it and this Braid managed to light and by the time he had got it going satisfactorily, Rachel came in with another armful of wood she had gathered up from the yard, then, he thought, just in the way that Bree would have done, put aside her coat and hat and set about making a meal. Braid's coffee pot was brought out and presently the rich smells of coffee and bacon pervaded the mean little room, a place of rough, bare boards and gaps in walls and roof. There were no bunks, in fact there was no furniture of any kind, and when the meal was ready they had to sit cross-legged on the floor to eat it, but after the wet wagon camps of recent weeks it seemed none too bad.

Braid looked across at the little heap of clothing that had been bought for Rachel.

"I hope it fits."

"It won't be too small, and I can alter anything that has to be altered," she said, and with a confidence that told him there could be no doubt about it. As though she had been reading his mind, she said: "Where we were, where my pa had his place, before it all went bad, we all had our things to do. Nobody could sit back. There was always too much that had to be done." He nodded. Even after all that effort, he thought, it had still got the better of Ben Olvie, the weather, the times, the prices, the predators of one sort or another. Braid knew quite well that out of habit, born no doubt of that daily, unflagging necessity she had just talked about, she had watched him at the camps, listened to him, and had absorbed not only his views but his likes and dislikes. She was indeed like her mother, getting the essential things done no matter what the difficulties might be. But for all that, mother and elder daughter had a certain way with them. In Rachel it was as much in the light way that she moved as anything else that caught the attention, for there was nothing remotely clumsy about her; and undeniably she was a girl to make any man look again. There was about her a slimness, a roundness, a lightness of step and of touch, an almost wafting presence that at once marked her out as distinctive; a gentleness, an unlikely product, some might think, of simple farm folk like the Olvies. She had very dark brown hair, worn to just below her shoulders, delicate black eyebrows, cool-looking, quite flawless, creamy skin, full, pink lips, a slim neck, narrow shoulders and small, high breasts and a very narrow waist, so that measuring it, a man's hands might seem almost to span it.

Riders had come. Though Braid had not heard them approaching, when he went out to look for more wood for the stove, he saw them arriving at the trading post, four of them. If they noticed him they offered no sign of it, disappearing around the front of the main building. Braid fossicked for wood, then went back into the shack.

She had taken the opportunity to try on the levis and shirt and was still buttoning the shirt when he came in and kicked the door shut with one foot. As she had predicted, the clothes were not too small for her but were not far off it and they presented Rachel as long-legged and tightly rounded. She was now bare-footed and she had tied on a broad, bright yellow headband around her forehead but tucked beneath her hair at the back. He did not want to stare at her, but when he dumped the wood down he said:

"You were right. They're fine. You look good."

She smiled, pleased, then said: "What's the matter?"

"Nothing." He moved his head slightly. "Some riders at Keast's. Just be careful if you go out."

She said; "Well, I'll have to go out. There's a privy in that yard?"

"Yes," Then: "I'll walk to a place where I can watch Keast's."

He did, though the light was now fading, and no-one came near. When she came back, she said: "Braid, that truly was an awful place. Any sign of anybody?"

"No. And there might not be, anyway. It's just that he sells liquor in there as well, an' you never do know how that might come out in a place like this." He glanced around. There was no lamp here, only the cherry glow from the pot-bellied stove. They put their bedrolls down on either side of the stove, as near to it as they thought prudent, and the saddles, and Braid found a piece of wood fortuitously shaped, and wedged it under the bottom of the door. When he had done that he sat on his bedroll and began taking his boots off, concentrating on the task, and he could hear the slithering of fabric as Rachel got her things off. He removed his outer clothes, and in longjohns, reached for his blanket. Rachel had the Indian blankets and when he looked he could see the shine of her dark eyes in the glow from the stove and one ivory shoulder, and was aware, in the instant, of the almost imperceptible shake of her head in the half-light.

"Not just yet, Braid. In time. In my own time."

He drew his blanket up and lowered his head down against the smooth saddle and within minutes both he and Rachel slept.

In the dawn he was dressed and with his shellbelt buckled and wearing his short coat when she came fumbling from sleep. He said: "I'll go see to the horses."

She propped on one elbow, hair hanging partly over her face, blankets drawn up under her chin, a small, hibernating animal now, blinking from its lair.

"Is it wet or dry out there?"

"Dry so far, I'd say, but cold."

She seemed to hug the blankets more snugly around her, as a child might. "I'll fix us something to eat."

He unwedged the door and went outside, feeling at once the sharp chill. Coming around the corner of the shack he became aware of the sound of voices in the still, grey morning, even before he saw a group of men outside the barn where the horses had been left.

Braid did not much fancy the looks of this and his first thought was that he was pleased that Rachel was not with him and he hoped that if she did come out and see them, she would go quietly back inside. He thought he himself was now too far into the open to retreat to warn her.

Keast was on hand, his short pudgy fingers shoved down inside his belt, and so too were his employees, a pair of nondescript individuals in dirty clothing, moleskin trousers and, even in the cold of the early day, pinkish woollen vests, much sweat-stained. And there were four others, range riders, probably those that Braid had noticed coming to the trading post on the previous evening and having perhaps spent most of the night drinking. All had cow-ponies with slung lariats and canteens, and all the men were hung with shellbelts and a variety of pistols in old holsters. They were wearing faded, coloured shirts in varying states of repair, bandannas of either blue or red and tall, wide-brimmed hats.

They had apparently not interested themselves in Braid's horse, but one of the cowmen had got hold of Half Moon's mane and had brought the chestnut out of the barn. Not too surprisingly, this man was having trouble holding the horse steady and in fact was being pulled about as Half Moon balked and snorted and tossed its head.

Braid was closing the distance. Keast had begun scratching slowly at his protruding belly, but noticing the steady approach of the big man whose fleece-lined coat was now open, exposing brass-shelled belt and the reddish-wood butt of a long pistol, he stopped doing it, conscious of a worm of unease. His men looked too, and one after another the range men, probably because something had been said, all except the one who was still trying to get Half Moon under control.

When Braid was about thirty feet from them he called clearly, though not loudly: "Let go the horse!" Somehow, without being obvious about it, they could not fail to see that the oncoming man had contrived to push back and secure his open coat so that the butt of the big pistol was fully exposed, indeed stood out, the man's hand almost brushing it as he walked.

Ten paces short of them, Braid stopped. Half Moon was still unsettled and the cowhand was still hanging on, grunting and tugging and sometimes being half dragged along. Again, Braid said: "Let go the horse!"

The man who had been trying to hold Half Moon let go and backed away. Braid's guess was that Keast would stand watching, simply to see what came out of this; and neither of Keast's men, by the looks of them, were up to much. Of the four range men two looked uncertain, appraising Braid, perhaps a touch disturbed by what they saw. The other two, a red-headed, stringy-necked fellow with mad, greenish eyes, and a more solidly-built, bearded man who stank worse than Keast, might well be a different matter; and so it soon became clear.

The man who stank said:

"I reckon this here horse come from Lefabor's Hook outfit down on the Wolverine. That's Lefabor's brand on it."

"Well," Braid said, "I shot the unfriendly bastard that had it right off the top of it, an' he was a few years ride from the Wolverine when I did it. That's my first an' last word on this horse. What about you?"

Seconds went by with only the white vapouring of breath among them, then the bearded man, having gone as far as he had, stuck to it doggedly.

"It still don't wash Lefabor's brand off, whatever yuh done, mister, or whoever he was that had it."

"That's damn' right," the red-haired man said in a high, shredded voice.

Braid knew that he had to finish it now before the other cowhands took courage and started putting their oars in; so to the bearded man he said: "Mister, not long from now, that horse is leaving here, an' it's leaving when

I leave. Now, if it's in your mind to put a rope on it, either in your name or in this Lefabor's name, then this is the time to do it, because I've not yet eaten an' I don't reckon to delay that long, either. So either tell your friend there to take hold of the horse again one way or another an' pay the price for doing it, or all back off an' go your own way. Now which is it to be?"

"It's four to one," the redhead put in, but his tone was not as confident as it had been.

"You want to be the party that gets it down to three to one?" Braid enquired, and then, to the bearded man: "Well come on, what's it to be?" Braid was standing quite still, right hand hanging slackly near the butt of the pistol.

After what seemed a long silence the bearded one gave a shrug. Braid was still aware of the stench of him. Blackbeard then made a movement with his head, turned away and mounted up. After the briefest of pauses his companions mounted and followed him. Yet it was not quite the last word for the bearded man drew rein to stare back at Braid. "I don't know who the hell yuh are, mister, but I still say yuh got bad habits with other people's horses."

Evidently Keast thought that at that, Braid might draw the pistol, for he said quickly, low-voiced and a touch hoarse; "Don't do it, mister, not on my place."

"Shit on your place," Braid said. Then: "You get these two boys here to saddle that horse an' saddle the black as well. I'm going to the shack to eat. Another thing, you'd best see those other bastards off your damn' place, for they'd do well not to be still around when I come out." He turned on his heel and began to walk away, then paused, half turning. "Where are they from?"

"Sutter's Three Diamond," said Keast, "'bout ten mile north o' here."

"What name does black whiskers go by?"

Keast shook his head and raised his bushy eyebrows. "Don't know no names."

Braid thought he was probably lying but did not press the matter. The four cowhands were still in sight, riding away.

Rachel had put on her riding clothes and he all but collided with her when he came around the corner of the shack. In some surprise, he asked: "Could you have shot that thing? It's got some punch."

"I don't know. I've only ever fired small calibre before. I watched you at the camp, how you held it. I don't know. It's heavy. Might be I'd only have let them see it." She looked down at the carbine in her small, long-fingered hands, then went into the shack. "I was just about to let you know that chow was ready when I saw them all there."

"It weighs eight an' a quarter pounds, a bit more with a full magazine, if you think that's heavy," said Braid.

"Who were they, those men?"

"Some long-nosed cowboys that couldn't mind their own damn' business. God knows why they went into that barn, looking at our horses, but one of 'em claimed Half Moon was off a ranch 'way down on the Wolverine, the Hook. Maybe he is. Anyway, I told 'em we weren't about to give him up to them, an' I asked 'em to leave."

She paused, coffee pot in hand. "And they went, just like that?"

"Yeah, we'd run out of things to say. Can we eat now, an' be on our way?"

Seeing him as he was now, his imposing bulk, and having watched, albeit from a distance, the stand-off between Braid and the strangers, she believed she could understand how even range men such as those who had just left might be uncertain, even afraid of him. She decided, however, that she was not afraid of him.

4

THE sound of the rain on the roof was almost deafening. Braid was there, dripping, his hat and his slicker darkly bright with water, also a man who had given his name as Ridley, and whose lamp had been on in a freight depot, drawing them like moths to a candle in the cold, wet, sparsely-lit main street of Coldheart. And Lapin, the undertaker, was there of course. Rachel had balked at coming in though and had remained on the darkened back porch of the undertaker's establishment, the two wet-smelling horses hitched to the porch rail.

Lapin, at first moving around in the dark with the confidence of familiarity, had lit a lamp and though he had turned it up, the stark room they were in remained awash with shadows.

There were three trestle tables in the place, each holding a body covered with a sheet. Both Ridley and Lapin were wearing hats and long coats, and like Braid, were dripping onto the bare wooden floor. There was a musty, sweet-sour smell and an enclosing chill about the room, and a curiously cold, pinched look about the undertaker, Lapin, which seemed somehow appropriate to this stark environment. Ridley the freighter, a large man going to seed, apparently was not there simply because he happened to have been approached by strangers, giving him a name, but also because he had had some connection with the man Braid had come seeking in Coldheart.

Lapin, sniffing because of a headcold, lifted the end of one of the sheets and said in a rather husky voice: "This is him. This is Arn Bessemer." The exposed head and shoulders were those of a middle-aged man with thinning dark hair and a thick, dark moustache, the skin pale and sagging in death, and a bluish tinge to the lips, the eyelids closed. Lapin covered the face again. "Yesterday," Lapin said, "he got a bad pain in one arm and a couple of hours later he just fell down in the street." When Braid looked at him he added: "Heart." Lapin sniffed thoroughly.

"He had a bank here?" asked Braid. Ridley answered.

"Coldheart Bank and Loan," he said. "He was a partner. The other half is Bob Dalton." Wheezing slightly, Ridley gave his full attention to Braid and spoke up more because of the sound of the rain. "Arn Bessemer sent you word to come here."

"Yeah, but I've been a while getting to it. So, that's that."

"Arn said he'd heard about you. Took him a while to locate you. We agreed he'd be the one to send you word. We didn't hear nothin' back."

"We?"

"A few people here. Arn was a feller

that did things, got things movin'."

"So that's the reason I heard from just him."

"Yeah. Yeah, but there's others agreed at the time."

"Such as?"

"Oh well, me, an' Dalton of course at the bank. A man named Lowell, another called Moyle. Look Braid, it's a hell of a night an' it's a bad hour for talk. Why don't you an' — why don't you find someplace for a night's rest an' we'll talk some more tomorrow?"

Braid considered that he really had little option. Here they were, indeed at a late hour, the weather bad, tired from the trail, the man who had sent word to Braid lying here under a sheet, dead. But Braid, after the purchases at Keast's, had little money left, and perhaps something of his dilemma was betrayed by his expression, for Ridley then said:

"There's a barn back of the freight office an' a bunkhouse my drivers use sometimes, but none of 'em's there right now. You an' — you could use that." Ridley once again had seemed momentarily confused, remembering the girl who had arrived with Braid and who was still waiting outside. Clearly he had not known how to refer to her. Braid nodded, but before turning away, indicated the other two sheet-covered corpses.

"Who were they?"

"We don't know," Lapin said, sniffing again. He moved across, his shadow leaping grotesquely over the ceiling and pulled back one of the sheets. The man's head was a mass of dried black blood and one eye seemed to be missing. "Miners, we think," Lapin said, "waylaid and robbed for what they might have been carrying." He pulled the sheet up again.

"Why aren't they known? Don't they have kin around here?" Braid asked.

Lapin shrugged. "Not all of the miners we see here in town are from legitimate, registered Poison River claims. There are . . . itinerants as well.

I suppose you could call them poachers, not claim-jumpers as such. Thieves. They're only one of the problems we have in Coldheart."

"Well, if they were what you say, it looks like they met their match," Braid observed.

Lapin remained inside his sombre parlour when Ridley, followed by Braid, went out into the blustery rain. Braid and Rachel did not mount up again but, leading their horses, followed Ridley out of the yard, along an alley of water-filled ruts, then across Main to where a lamp still shone palely in the freight office, and down another wind-buffeted alley to another back yard, Ridley rattling bolts at one of the outhouses there.

"In here. There's a lamp an' a stove. Down to the left, yonder, there's a barn for your horses." Braid had half expected Rachel to ask where the privy was but she didn't because they could all smell where it was. "I'll leave you, then," said Ridley, and he went away through the soaking darkness, his boots squelching.

Braid went into the small bunkhouse, found the lamp and lit it, then with Rachel and Half Moon following him, walked the black along in mud, through the pelting rain to the barn.

Half an hour later they were back in the bunkhouse, Braid lighting the iron stove, and Rachel, struggling out of her coat, said: "Was that him in there? The man Bessemer?"

"That's what they say. He fell over dead."

"So what happens now? Do we move on, go back? Or what?"

"The man who brought us around here, Ridley, wants to talk. Tomorrow. And there'll be others with him. We'll have to see. Got to find work somewhere, an' soon."

"Braid, was it a mistake to bring me along?"

"No. No it wasn't, Rachel."

In the morning, although the rain had eased to intermittent showers, everything was still dripping and the air was still cuttingly cold, so when at mid-morning Ridley called out to Braid, Rachel elected to remain in the bunkhouse near the stove until the outcome of the meeting should be known.

At the back of Ridley's large freight building was a nearly bare room and it was to this that Ridley led Braid, who was surprised by the number of people already there. They had been talking animatedly among themselves but when Ridley entered and behind him Braid filled the doorway, they fell silent. Ridley at once introduced to Braid several of those present. Braid shook no hand, merely nodding to each in turn.

"Bob Dalton." A middle-sized, pale man dressed rather formally and wearing a large wine-coloured cravat. The banker, partner of the late Arn Bessemer.

"Dave Lowell." A tall, bony, narrow-faced man, well attired, with an expensive-looking, silver-scrolled waistcoat and gold watch-chain. This was the owner of one of Coldheart's three saloons.

"Lapin, you already know." At that, a few eyebrows lifted but Ridley did not elaborate.

"Ed Moyle. Ed trades in anything that's tradeable." Round-faced, he was, inclining to ruddiness, with veined cheeks and small, brown-button eyes.

A tallish man with a finely-clipped moustache had come in late and was given passage to advance to the front of the group, a man with a direct gaze and one of whose legs seemed to be stiff.

"Major Brooke," Ridley said, "surgeon." What might have inspired an ex-army surgeon with the rank of major to choose a town such as Coldheart in which to practise, Braid could but speculate upon, but he nodded, acknowledging him.

"And my wife, Alice." She was small, darkhaired, a good-looking woman with a dark blue cape over her neat, square shoulders, a woman Braid estimated to be a good ten years younger than Ridley, and she regarded Braid steadily out of large eyes that very nearly matched the colour of her cape.

There were others present, several men and some women, wives presumably, some in hooded capes like Alice Ridley, some wearing damp bonnets. All present looked to Ridley to do the initial talking amid the pervasive, musty smell of outer clothing seldom properly dried out.

"These people who've come here," Ridley explained, "are some of the citizens of Coldheart concerned enough about dangerous violence here to want to hire a man to be marshal." Expressionless, Braid listened, thinking that *concerned* fell a bit short of reality; they appeared to him as frightened people. No matter what words were spoken, there was always something else that found its way into the eyes, that was the giveaway. "For every man and woman here," Ridley went on, "there's another dozen that would be here if this place was big enough." There was a murmuring of assent but Ridley now paused, noticing that Braid was ready to ask a question.

"How long since there was any law here, an' exactly why isn't there now?" Braid asked.

"It's been about a year," said Ridley. "Dave Rochefort. A good man. A hard man that had his ways and his rules an' tried to see to it that the rules were kept. Some of it didn't sit well at all with some o' the hard-noses we allers get through this place. Marshal, well, it ain't an easy job. Maybe I don't have to tell you that. So Dave had problems. Anyway, in the finish, it all blew up in his face. He run a couple of real bad bastards out of Coldheart. Not long after, he got back-shot. He had no chance."

Braid had never heard of Rochefort. "A year is some while," he said.

"It's too damn' long." This was not Ridley but the ex-army surgeon speaking up; but he did add: "Which is not to say there's been no interest in replacing Rachefort sooner than this. But we could see it was no task for any of *us*. What's needed is a man with experience in doing the job. Arn Bessemer claimed he'd heard you well spoken of in other places at various times. That's how it was Bessemer came to send you word."

Braid made no comment to that. Whether or not the assembled people now liked what they saw standing before them he had no way of judging, for there was little animation about any of them, only what he read as apprehension. Except perhaps for Alice Ridley who seemed more at ease than anyone else there, as though she might only be present out of idle interest rather than the deep concern that Ridley had spoken of. Braid did cock an ear and gave them a frosty smile.

"I don't hear gunshots in the town."

"Stay more'n a few days an' you will," Moyle, the trader put in. One of the bonneted women in the group said:

"If there was less liquor there'd be a lot less trouble."

"We'd all agree on that," the banker, Dalton said.

That was the cue for the saloon-keeper, Lowell, to make some sort of defence for his own enterprise. He had been about to light a cigar, but now he hesitated.

"My employees do what they can to calm things down if they look like gettin' too far out of hand. I don't want my men or my furniture broke up any more than Sands does in the Blue Chip or Thomas at the Three Deuces. I'm not here to talk for them, but that I do know. It stands to reason."

Braid thought he might just as well make an observation that fell about in the middle of these two views, so he said:

"What the lady there said makes plenty of sense." The woman looked suitably righteous when others glanced at her. Lowell again paused in dealing with his cigar. "However," Braid went on, "saloons are part of business anywhere you go. They can be run well, or not. I did see a town, one time, that went as far as voting saloon doors shut. Liquor still came in, an' it was sold by scum that the saloons would've thrown out. First look, it sounds like a smart idea but I'd be prepared to say it doesn't work."

Lowell calmly lit his cigar. Ridley again took up the talk.

"Coldheart," he said, "is a mixture of cattle-town an' mine-town. There never was a bonanza up along the Poison River but there's plenty of good claims that are still bein' worked an' will be for a good long while; but for every good one, there's two, three poor ones an' others that were never up to much an' are plain worked out. That's led to friction not only up there but in town as well. But the worst trouble we have is when riders from the ranches are here when miners are here too, sort of in numbers. Especially any miners with pay-dirt to throw around. Things ain't none too good for beef. Some of the greasy sack outfits don't pay their men on due time, an' not much when they do pay. The biggest of the outfits, though, is Ord Curry's, an' Ord still pays his boys reg'lar. But Ord's foreman, man named Hart, he's got somethin' of a down on miners as a breed, so when he's in Coldheart an' miners are, that don't help."

Thus they traversed their troubles for a further ten minutes until they began repeating themselves; until in fact Dalton, in a clear voice, asked why they could not now agree on an offer to Mr Braid here, for the duties of peacekeeping for one year, wages to be paid out by the Coldheart Bank and Loan, funded in turn, as previously discussed, by contributions from the majority of the town's business concerns. So they did, offering eighty a month plus his accommodation, an offer which Braid declined, saying he would consider a hundred a month, the first month to be half in advance, plus allowance for food, plus accommodation for two people.

That was the point at which there fell an awkward quiet over a meeting which had seemed to be getting somewhere. News of the presence of the girl had obviously spread, and now they were uncertain what to say. The mouths of all the women there, with the sole exception of Alice Ridley, had tightened, and none of the men wanted to look directly at Braid. Finally, clearing his throat, Ridley said:

"When Bessemer sent you word, I reckon he . . . nobody expected . . . "

Deliberately, Braid allowed Ridley to trail off, plainly in some discomfort. Then Dalton said:

"There are some rooms behind and above the jailhouse, but they are kind of small, so . . . " He too trailed off uncertainly.

Braid nodded slowly. "If any of this

is a problem, there's not a lot of point in talkin' any more." And he began to turn away.

Taken aback, they concluded at once that he meant it. It took them but another half minute to sweep aside all matters seen as possible problems only moments before; they agreed to his terms, saying that if the accommodation were to prove inadequate, then something other would be found. But he had not yet done. "One thing more," said Braid, and now most of them were looking very wary indeed. "If it's as bad as you've told me it is, then there'll need to be firmness used, maybe even more than Rochefort used. Any consequences of that are my concern. The way I'll do things might not be to everybody's taste. Better to hear that now than worry about it later. In places like Coldheart, where there's gold to be had, where there's haves an' have-nots, an' some want to drink their wages, there'll be violence. You've told me that's why I'm standing here now. Sometimes violence has got to be matched by violence. I'll not stand for having my hands tied. That's all I've got to say."

As soon as Ridley had produced the keys to the jail and its accommodation and explained where to locate it, Braid left and went to acquaint Rachel of the outcome, news which she at first received with an engaging smile, for Braid did appear to be well satisfied. Then, more soberly, and with an almost uncanny perception, she enquired: "Did they ask about me?"

"Not exactly."

If she did not know what to make of that, then she did not pursue it either, asking instead: "Where will we live?"

"At the place where the town jail is. There's rooms, as well, an' I've got the keys."

They chose to ride the horses, for there was mud everywhere, and they thought it had been a mistake not to do so on the previous night; so Braid saddled up, loaded saddlebags, canteens and bedrolls and they walked the animals out of Ridley's yard and along the alley.

When they came out onto a bleak main street they paused, for a little way along to their right, on the boardwalk in front of the freight building, they could see the remnants of the group that had been at the meeting. Emerging, the townsfolk had clearly been persuaded to stand for a few minutes while, head beneath a black cloth, his large wooden camera on a tripod, an itinerant photographer recorded what he viewed as a typical scene for posterity. His powder flashed with sudden, artificial brightness. Rachel, muttering to herself, had to steady Half Moon before she and Braid went on their way, regarded in silence by the group in front of the freighter's.

When they got far enough away, the horses sloshing through yellowish mud, she said to his broad back: "They might've welcomed you here, Braid, maybe even enticed you a bit, but their eyes say something else."

"They need us."

"They need you."

"There's the jailhouse, over there," he said.

5

FROM his upper window Braid could observe how the new day came slowly to a bleak Coldheart. Still not fully dressed, he stood looking out across a place whose sharpness of roof and corner and chimney was still blurred by a seeming reluctance of the dark to depart, and where streets, as far as he could perceive, were still unstirring under a louring sky.

Now that he could view it from this elevated place he was struck by the size of the town, but if what he was looking at was a manifestation of human hopes as well as the product of commercial necessity, then Braid considered that it fell some way short of what his own expectations would have been; for what he could see was not in any particular way appealing to the eye: a mass of wet rooftops gleaming dully, a host of straight, narrow chimney pipes, many giving out smoke which, instead of climbing towards the low clouds, was hanging all across Coldheart like a pale blue gauze, the acrid sharpness of it penetrating the room he was in; and he would remember this smell whenever, in time to come, he cast his mind back to his time in this town.

Quietly he drew on the remainder of his clothes and his boots, and with a glance towards Rachel, still sleeping, reached for shellbelt and holster and prepared to go downstairs. He did pause again though, to look down at the small, gently-breathing girl, and had the sense that his life had changed markedly since the first uncomfortable hours they had passed in Coldheart, as had hers.

Together they had appraised the rooms where, in the forseeable future, they were to live, and inspected too, the dusty office that fronted the building and, in a short internal passageway, the two barred cells (which Rachel had referred to as the cages) behind it. Beyond another brief corridor was a long room equipped with cupboards, benches, a pot-bellied stove, a bare wooden table and several straight-backed chairs, a spartan place unrelieved by decoration of any kind and containing only random evidence of previous tenancy, some lamps, a few pitchers, a vessel for heating water, some cutlery going green. Through a door at the far end of this room was an annexe in which, surprisingly, stood an iron tub; and there was yet another door out of there which, as did the kitchen door, gave into a yard. Against one wall of the long kitchen was a flight of narrow, bare wooden stairs leading to a single room with an iron-framed bed in it, a wash-stand, a bowl and pitcher, a lamp and a curtained corner beyond which were several wall-hooks and hangers for clothes.

Around the yard stood several small outbuildings, a depressing-looking privy among them, and nearest the back door, what turned out to be a pumphouse, yielding when Braid tried the pump-handle, and after a spew of siltiness, a stream of cold, clear water. There was a small barn containing a trough long-since dried up, some old sacks of rotted feed, and all across the hard-packed, earthen floor a carpet of dirty brown straw.

Braid had installed the horses in the barn, unsaddled them and carried everything that was to be carried into the living-quarters. In one of the cupboards, shuddering at spiders, Rachel had found a broom and had lost no time putting it to use, then getting the stove going and heating water for the tub. Braid observed that there was about her a light briskness, a sense of what ought to be done, as though she might have been assembling in her mind long before arriving in this place or could ever have been certain that they would get here, an ordered succession of matters to be attended to. As Bree would have done.

Braid had gone out and picked up his advance from Dalton, then to Rachel's requirements, bought food, coming back to find that the table, chairs and floor had been washed down. He went out a second time, buying soap, extra blankets, towels and fuel for the lamps; and on a third trip, a sack of fresh feed for the horses.

After supper Rachel had heated water for a tub and had then disappeared into the annexe where she had remained for an hour, emerging wearing what once might have been Bree's robe over her nightdress and suggesting that Braid now empty and refill the tub. "When both of us stank, it didn't matter." As she had begun to go up the stairs she had said something else and it was not until her bare feet were vanishing from sight that he realized that it had been: "Don't be too long."

She had lain unmoving, facing away, but the near-side of the bed had had the blankets turned back. She had not stirred even when, lamp turned down, Braid now bathed and shaved, had eased his weight down onto the creaking bed.

In the faintest uncurtained window-glow, in the new darkness, Braid had felt that he was sliding into the slow preliminaries that began to invade the mind when sleep was approaching, yet a mysteriously populated dark whose confusing interplays had no coherence. He had been conveyed back in time to a place where he could see the Finder running but could not hear it, could discern rain lashing down but could not feel it, see the bedraggled figure of Olvie turning to say something but could not understand him. Bending to submerged spokes, Bree standing between the heads of the wagon-horses, her shabby skirts flapping with heavy soddenness in a gusting wind, but wind that curiously had now lost its power to chill him.

Slowly, almost silently, another figure detached itself from nearby gloom, but the rain, the wind, the wagon and the Olvies had vanished and he had realized then, coming to half wakefulness, that they had never existed where he now lay. He would have struggled to sit up but a butterfly touch of fingers had alighted on his mouth and his newly-shaven chin. Blankets had stirred, tugged. She had said nothing but he had perceived, though faintly, the slim, unclothed outline of her and under his hard hands, close to him, her firmness, her lithe, silken smoothness, her hair hanging forward over her narrow shoulders, her breath on his cheek, and he was conscious of the new soap smell about her. '*In my own time*,' she had said when they had been at Keast's.

He did not wake her now, pale young face, rich brown hair splayed wildly, but for an instant, just before he went downstairs, he experienced a sudden recall of the wagon near the Finder River and almost heard again a small boy's call: "*See yuh tomorrow, Rache*!" And long after they had vanished, Bree perhaps — Olvie waiting for her impatiently — hanging back a few minutes at the camp-site on some flimsy pretext, but looking for last footprints. He went out of the room.

Awakening like a kitten, with trembling stretches, she had heard him going down, doing his best to be quiet.

Braid had put on his warm jacket and in the dawn made his way along Main on the boardwalk, picking his way across the muddy outlets of sidestreets and alleys, looking along each one as he did so. On Main itself he noted where the saloons stood, the Blue Chip, the Three Deuces and the third, the Lucky Wheel, which must be Lowell's. The town was a conglomeration, reflecting its dual role. There were a number of streets and as he had observed from his upper window, a forest of chimneys; there were hotels and rooming-houses, barns and lumber yards and corrals. On a three-way corner stood the bank and loan; there were two general stores, a feed and grain, a barber's and all manner of small traders. The doctor's surgery, he noted, was located above one of the assay offices and accessed by an external stairway. There was another freighting outfit besides Ridley's, a gunsmith, a saddler, a blacksmith, a wheelwright, a cooper; and a shop-front now boarded up: THE COLDHEART ECHO. At one end of the town, a little apart from the other structures stood a small schoolhouse, while at the opposite end of Main, also a short distance away, a narrow building whose sign said: MINING EQUIPMENT: EXPLOSIVES. And beyond that, well beyond, perhaps two hundred yards, a collection of sad-looking shacks, almost as though the town might have begun to develop in that area, then changed its mind. Braid could see no church nor any place that said telegraph. Once in Coldheart, presumably, you were on your own in more ways than one.

When he came opposite Ridley's he

could see the freighter working inside his office under a yellow lamp, and when Ridley glanced up and noticed him, he stepped into his doorway. Braid crossed the rutted, muddy street.

"You're out an' about early," Ridley observed.

"Looking at how the land lies," said Braid.

"There's a badge," Ridley remarked, "that was Rochefort's. Not sure where. Maybe around that office down there."

"I'll look," Braid said. Then he nodded towards the outer buildings. "Beyond that mining equipment outfit," he said, "there's some shacks. Anybody live there?"

"That's where the whores are," Ridley said, "but you won't need to concern yourself with them."

"How so?"

"The town limit is the far side of Halloran's Mining. The whores ain't part of Coldheart."

"What about their customers?" asked Braid. "Don't any of 'em live here?"

Ridley looked briefly uncomfortable. "Look," he said, "we made a point of keepin' the whores out of Coldheart. What goes on in the Cribs ain't our concern."

Braid considered the distance afresh, deciding that his first estimate of two hundred yards had been generous.

"This must mean," he said, "that the gold claims up along the Poison River an' anything that might happen there, are none of my concern either."

"Well now," Ridley said, "understand that there's women an' kids up there too. Rochefort saw it as his duty to keep an eye out among the miners." Ridley seemed to be floundering to some extent, but then he said: "It wouldn't set too well to get too interested in the Cribs. The women here are kinda touchy about the whores bein' as close as that as it is."

Braid digested that, thinking that he would not push the matter any further at the moment, but he did observe: "I don't see a church here. That's not usual."

"There was one, years back," said Ridley, "but it got burned down. The preacher turned out not to be safe around kids. He's probably still runnin'. Nobody else come. They do hold prayer meetin's here an' there. Groups."

When Braid went back to the jailhouse he could smell the rich aroma of breakfast before he went in the door. She was flitting busily about, not looking at him particularly, as though this were all a part of some long-established routine. He told her what Ridley had said about what he had referred to as the Cribs, and about town limits and the mine camps.

"You don't approve of some part of your town," he said, "you draw a line short of it an' pretend it's not there."

"What will you do?"

He shrugged. "Take things as they come. One thing's sure though, whether Ridley or anybody else here knows it or not; fail to be seen to be the law when you've got the badge on, an' you're as good as dead."

A little later he did find the badge that Ridley had spoken of in a drawer in the old desk up in the office, a dented, dulled star, the word MARSHAL barely discernible. He pinned it to his jacket.

In early evening, in a long room under smoky lamps, amid voices and laughter, somebody said: "Marshal? What marshal?"

"The one that's just walked in."

Voices did not die away altogether but some hands of cards were lowered, and groups around the whirling wheels turned to look at him.

"Who is he?"

"Name of Braid. Come in yesterday. With some girl or other."

"He's a big bastard."

Braid nodded to Lowell but declined the offer of a drink and did not stay long, going out again into the night, shrugging a little in his thick coat, for the wind, as well as being cold, was carrying fine rain. But he stuck to his task, even going through back streets before returning to Main, standing a moment or two under an overhanging verandah outside the gunsmith's at the top end of the street. He was about to turn and walk away when heard the ragged scream borne on the wind and his head went up like some old hunting dog, alert to see where the bird would fall.

6

SOMEBODY had slid a bolt across, inside, so Braid swung a boot up. The door of the shack was flimsy and crashed open, shuddering, giving off fine dust, and then Braid, with explosive speed for a big man, was inside. The ivory-skinned whore was struggling to her knees in a mess of porcelain from a smashed pitcher, water splashed everywhere, her breasts pendulous, bright blood on her face. A heavily-moustached man clad only in a grey shirt was standing over her, but now half turned, eyes under bushy brows widening at the banging open of the door and the sudden appearance of Braid.

"Back off her," Braid said. Caught as he was, the moustached man did so, retreating until he fetched up against a wall. The whore was moaning now and racked with gulping sobs, head drooping, hair cast forward over her face, blood and saliva threading down from mouth and nose.

Braid went to her, his boots crunching on pieces of porcelain, reaching down one broad hand, helping her to stand, then supporting her until she could sit on the rumpled bed. When the man made as though to move, Braid looked at him. "You're begging to have your mouth busted." Movement ceased. To the whore Braid said: "Has he paid you?" A slight shake of the head, face still buried in long black hair. Braid glanced around, then picked up the man's discarded pants. In one of the pockets he found several crumpled bills and tossed them onto the bed. "She'll need plenty for the surgeon." He then threw the pants, a pair of longjohns, socks and boots at the man's feet. "Put 'em on, then get out. Henceforth keep clear of this place, this girl." Then, because this man did not look like a cowhand: "Where are you from?

The claims?" A nod of the head. "Who are you?" When there was no response, Braid repeated, louder: "Who are you?"

"Sholto."

"You understand what I've told you, Sholto?"

"Who the hell *are* yuh?" It was not quite bluster, but now, almost clothed, his confidence was returning, his deep humiliation biting.

"I'm what this badge says I am. The name's Braid. Remember it, for I'll sure remember yours. Now get." When with a last malevolent glance, Sholto had gone, Braid looked more closely at the whore's injuries. Her lower lip was cut and she thought that one of her teeth had been broken. He straightened up. "I'll have the surgeon come," he said. She shook her head slightly.

"That army John? He won't come here."

"He'll come."

As he was leaving, light streaming

from other doorways as other whores looked out, he thought he caught sight of someone hurrying away towards the town and felt sure that it was not Sholto. The wrong build. It had been only a glimpse but he believed it had looked more like the round-faced man, Moyle, the one Ridley had said traded in anything tradeable.

The whore must have known something. Major Brooke did not give the impression that he wanted to go down to the Cribs. Braid, at the top of the stairs outside the building had had to hammer on the door before eventually it was opened by Brooke clad in night-clothes. Braid was crisply invited in, principally, he thought, because the open door was letting in the night's cold.

When Braid told him why he was there, some of the early prickliness went away and Brooke appeared less assertive, even discomfited, clearly wanting to say neither yes nor no.

"One of the er, women there, you say?"

"Yeah, she ran up against a bastard that likes to slap the girls around. She might be missing a tooth an' there's no doubt she's got a cut lip."

"It's damn' late," said Brooke, back to his snappy tone.

"That's when the girls do most business," Braid said. He could see Brooke's bright, dark eyes glittering in the glow of a single, subdued lamp. "I'll wait," said Braid. Brooke hesitated a few more seconds, then said quite brusquely:

"Give me five minutes."

"Later," Rachel said: "You mean he really didn't want to go?"

"He didn't, but he didn't want to say it to me," Braid said. "But he did go, and once he got there he sure knew what he was doing."

Unexpectedly Rachel asked: "What was her name?"

"Greta."

To Braid's mild surprise nobody in

the town mentioned the technicalities of the town limits and his getting involved, as marshal, in what had happened at the Cribs, though the opportunity was there the next day when he spoke, in passing, to both Ridley and Dalton; but Braid could see by the way they looked at him, almost as though seeing him for the first time, that there might well be things they would have liked to have said but for some reason had held back.

He had left money with Rachel and when he returned to the jail office he discovered her swabbing floors and passageways with a new mop.

"And I found which keys opened the cages," she said, "so now a person can breathe in there, too." Indeed he found that there was a definite carbolic atmosphere about the place and that the rank smell that earlier had been evident had dissipated. And later, just before supper, she remarked: "And I bought this." She slipped on a bright red and white headband which, like the yellow one she had bought at Keast's gave her a faintly Indian appearance. "And these." Definitely Indian; bright, soft moccasins. "And see, a new house dress." Holding it up for his approval, fine yellow-and-white checkers. "Oh, and I went to see Greta."

"What's that you say?"

"Greta, the . . . girl who got hurt. I made some broth and took it up there. I thought her face would be too puffed up for her to eat regular food." When his arms enclosed her quite narrow shoulders the dark eyes seemed to grow even larger, more luminous. "Did I do wrong?"

"Not in my book," he said, "but then, I'm a deeply prejudiced man." Releasing her, he gave her small bottom a slap. "Let's eat." She went skipping lightly away from him, giggling.

But the next time she returned from Main with provisions she seemed withdrawn, pensive, and when he asked her if anything was the matter, she avoided answering until he rose and came across and put his hands gently on her shoulders.

"What is it that's been said, Rache?"

She shook her head. "Maybe it's just me. I can feel when folk don't approve. I mean, I think I can."

"Who? Men? Women? Who?"

"The women, mostly." Then quickly she added: "Nothing *said*. Just the way some of them look. Talk, too, I'd say, after I've gone by."

"You will take broth to whores." But he knew that was not the entire reason.

She laughed and pressed her head against him. *Braid's girl*. Invariably they said *Braid's girl*, not *Braid's woman*. But no-one said anything outright either to Braid or to her.

Soon, Braid himself became a familiar figure in Coldheart. He did not, as some thought he might, haunt the saloons, but he did look in on them from time to time, making it clear by his attitude as much as by anything he said, that he would not concern himself with every minor scuffle, but: "If things turn real bad, I'll be there." Whenever the horses of range riders were to be seen hitched along Main in numbers, he did go in to give their riders some scrutiny; and on one of these visits saw among them a powerful, dark-haired man, the C-Star foreman, Hart, who looked back hard and unflinchingly at Braid, but did not speak. Yet in that glance Braid was aware that he was being sized up, that Hart and those with him had been discussing him.

Braid, too, was frequently to be seen on the streets, the back streets as well as Main, walking casually yet storing away in his mind every yard, every building, every alleyway; and there were plenty of people in the town who drew reassurance simply from his strong, composed-looking presence. In particular and not surprisingly, the women. He sensed all this, sometimes half-heard it, while maintaining a firm though courteous distance, this in spite of interest, albeit necessarily reserved, from one or two of them; the timid, pale girl, Maria Lutyens for one, whose eyes with their faintly dark rings lingered on him; and there was a detached but unmistakeable and therefore disturbing appraisal by Alice Ridley.

Not too long after Braid had taken the job on, Dalton, plainly a reticent man, had felt moved to say to him: "Just having law here again, visible day and night, is letting everybody sleep easier."

Braid had acknowledged that but at the same time had sounded a caution. "I've hardly got started, an' I've not yet been pushed. When I am, an' I will be, we'll see how things stand."

Still nobody came right out and mentioned Rachel to him, as though there might have been a universal — and agreed — covenant not to do so for fear of provoking him. For her part, Rachel went about her affairs, in and out of the Coldheart stores, self-contained, preoccupied. Privately, to Braid, she revealed a younger-seeming vulnerable self. She had a way of biting her lower lip when she was uncertain or apprehensive, and another unconscious habit of rubbing one ankle slowly against the other calf, as a very young girl might do, an action which both irritated and in an odd way warmed him. And occasionally, in the middle of busy tasks, composed and confident, she was moved suddenly to say something like: "You'll take good care, Braid, won't you?" He was equally protective of her, counselling continual caution, instilling an unvarying routine.

"If you're going to stay in this part of the place when I'm out, lock the front door to the office as well as the back door. If there's anybody in the, er, cages, don't ever forget yourself an' move too close to the bars."

Because, however, nothing very serious seemed to be happening, she did once remark: "This Coldheart, it doesn't seem to be as bad as they told you it was."

"Then you can be sure it isn't what it seems. In a town like this, believing there isn't any danger could fetch us both up in Lapin's parlour."

When he went out after dark, surveying the town's activities, he made sure that Rachel performed all the locking up behind him, and always left the carbine near her.

"I still don't know if I could shoot it."

"Anybody coming in won't know that."

People he passed on these solitary walks, going often through spilled lamplight, nodded to him, spoke, some of them. He kicked drunks homeward, confronted any who were themselves in confrontation, cleared them off the streets, walked on in the cold air, breath vapouring. Not all of those he met seemed well disposed towards him. Buying ammunition in Lutyens' and while he was there, looking at guns, putting them back in the racks, the bony-faced gunsmith regarded him from sunken sockets.

"Don't be all night about it. I want to close up."

Walking out, catching sight of Maria Lutyens' wan face beyond a pulled-back door-curtain, until her father looked and saw her and the curtain fell back into place. A widower, so Braid understood, Lutyens, surly, all his good years gone, with his rundown shop in a Godforsaken town, with his sad girl.

Braid moved around back streets where unseen dogs barked, passing briefly near the back of Moyle's house, having heard the determined singing of women long before he came abreast of the place.

'In grief and fear to Thee O Lord,
We now for succour fly;
Thine awful judgements are abroad,
O shield us lest we die.'

A throwing up of barricades against possible invaders, ancient fears; the crucifix, the clove of garlic. *The louder we sing, the safer we shall be*. Freda Moyle and her prayer meeting, the husband presumably elsewhere.

And twice in recent times, coming incomprehensibly from a dark and desolate area of Coldheart, walking quickly as though, Braid thought, wanting to distance himself from something, the banker, Dalton. A precise, fussy man, in a sense like the surgeon, Major Brooke, but without Brooke's brusque army manner.

Going on past Ridley's where living quarters were above the freight office, seeing faint lights behind curtains his thoughts turned to Alice Ridley. He had encountered her casually two or three times and she had been at pains to make sure that he paused to talk to her; mundane talk, as it had turned out, innocuous, but avoiding any mention whatsoever of Rachel. Lifting his hat, moving on, he had been under no illusion, however, about what Alice's striking cobalt eyes had really been saying to him. Once, coming home, he had said to Rachel: "I spoke with Ridley's wife. Do you know her?"

"Alice Ridley," Rachel said. "No, but I've seen her. I know who she is. She's fond of men, I think."

"What makes you say that?"

Rachel had shrugged. "Just watching her." Then, grinning wickedly, had added: "Maybe she's setting her cap at you, Braid."

He had hooked his arm around her slim neck and caught her head into his chest, Rachel performing a charade of trying to escape. "If she is," Braid promised, "then she'd best prepare to be disappointed."

Saturday night. Horses were hitched outside all of the Coldheart saloons. Inside, wheels were spinning, cards flicking brightly under smoky lamps, and the noise, overlaid by the tinkling of tinny pianos, could be heard wherever you were on Main and even beyond. A few minutes after eight o'clock, in the Blue Chip, one of Curry's C-Star riders by the name of Snell collided with a drummer from Phoenix and Snell at once took exception and hit him. The drummer went backwards taking a card table and its contents with him, putting the players also into disarray, two of them falling to the floor with the drummer. The other two rounded on Snell, whose several C-Star companions now closed in to his support. Harve Sands, whose establishment this was, two of his Bar Dogs with him, and all armed with pick handles, came vaulting over the bar, Sands red-faced and shouting for order. Glasses smashed and another table upended.

Precisely when Braid arrived could not afterwards be recalled but as soon as he saw him there Sands waved his men back. "*Marshal!*" Another man, C-Star, backed off with them, but the first the rest of them knew about it was when Braid was among them, seizing, shoving, with the benefit of sobriety, making his strength and his weight felt. Only Snell, who had started it, seemed set to resist, but Braid's big left hand bunched the front of Snell's shirt and the right one slapped with the sound of a whiplash across his face. Braid shoved him away, clumping him against the bar, men scattering, then punched him solidly in the midriff, jack-knifing him, driving the breath out of him. Now the considerable noise had all gone draining away.

"Whoever it was began this," Braid said, "pays the damages." Sands nodded briefly towards the gasping Snell. "So be it," Braid said, then held one hand up, glancing around at serious, flushed, angry, apprehensive faces under the smoke-haze. "The new Coldheart rules," he said, "are that nobody that causes damage walks away from it. Recompense is made. It's full an' it's immediate." To Sands, he said: "He pays before he walks out of the door. If not, he's in the cells." Sands nodded but ventured the thought that Snell might not have the price of it. "Then his friends," Braid said, "if that's what these monkeys here are, can rally to his need. I don't give a shit how he finds the money but before he leaves, he pays. If it should come to it, I'll have his fly-blown horse out there an' sell that to pay."

"The hell you will mister." Unnoticed, the dark man, Hart, had come in. Almost as tall as Braid, compact and muscular, he was plainly not a man to look away from another, or who would show any inclination to back down; Curry's foreman, accustomed to handling the hard characters who, year by year worked cattle. "The hell yuh will, mister, I don't know where in the name o' God this dump found yuh, but yuh sure do have a lot to learn."

Braid faced him. Snell, supporting himself on the bar, was in no great shape. The other C-Star men were still standing back but now that Hart had arrived their faces were saying: *This is where this Goddamn' mouthy bastard gets leg-roped*. To his credit, Sands said:

"Your man Snell, here, he started it, an' all out o' nothin'."

Hart bent his dark gaze on him.

"What? A lousy chair or two? A table? A few glasses? Listen, Sands, C-Star wages that's come across your cesspool of a bar have already paid for this whole dump even if it got *burned* down." And to Braid, again: "So yuh pumped the breath out of my rider, here, so that's it. We're all square, C-Star an' Coldheart. Let there be no more talk of payment, an' in particular, let there be no talk at all of cells an' of horses bein' seized, yuh hear?"

Braid fronted him more closely. "I can see it now," he said, "you're deaf. Your boy here is a shit-mad saddlebum that can't hold his liquor, hired on by a foreman that's stone deaf. So now cup your ear. Your boy pays the damages or he spends as much time holding onto *my* bars as it takes until the breakage is made good; an' if I've a mind to seize the animal he managed to ride here on, to make that happen, then that's what I'll do. You an' the rest of these imitation hard-men can either accept that or get your shiny asses out of Coldheart an' stay out." Before Hart could react to that, another waft of cold air came in with a thickset, florid man wearing a heavy jacket not unlike Braid's.

"What in the name o' God's goin' on here? Hart?" This was Ord Curry of C-Star.

"Sweet Jesus," said Braid, "don't tell me I've got to say it all again."

Sands spoke up, explaining to Curry what had happened. Curry gave the impression that he had had a difficult day and now did not need this damn' nonsense. He took out a wallet and passed some bills to Sands. "Don't get the idea that I'm payin' for this. I'll stop it out of his wages." He jerked his head towards Snell and the other C-Star men to indicate that that was the end of it, but to Braid, he said: "So we got the law here again. It's been some while. Just so yuh don't lean on my boys too hard. They work their asses off, because they work for me, an' they ain't none of 'em come out of a Mission."

"Granted," said Braid. "But when they're here in Coldheart they're answerable to me. They want to bust some place up, they'll have to make do with your bunkhouse."

Curry's flinty eyes examined Braid closely. "So be it, but you make real sure yuh put the same bootheel on the bastards from up along them claims, for another thing is that my boys don't take to bein' provoked."

Braid smiled, but mirthlessly. "If it's one thing we are more than another these days in Coldheart," he said, "it's even-handed."

Curry walked away, Hart following, Braid following him. Outside on the boardwalk, Hart lingered, clearly still filled with tight anger, and unafraid. "Don't think that'll be the finish of it mister." He moved away to the horses where Curry was mounting up, the rest of the C-Star crew preparing to do likewise. The drummer came out holding a bandanna to his mouth, and Braid told him where he might find Brooke; then Braid rubbed his hands together and strolled the cold streets for a while.

When he got home Rachel would not open the door until she heard his voice.

"I heard somebody. A while ago, in the yard. I turned the lamp out and looked out the window. I think I saw somebody there, but whoever it was went away. Was it you? Did you come back, earlier?" He shook his head. He went out and checked all around, searched every outbuilding, spent time in the barn looking over the horses and making sure nobody was hiding there. He felt unsettled. Maybe somebody had watched him go out, waited. Again he counselled Rachel to take great care.

7

THEY had ridden some way along the Poison River, climbing into the uplands above Coldheart, though not pressing on as far as the gold claims. However they could see many shacks all overlaid by chimney smoke, and this flat blanket of smoke went reaching a long distance up through the high, dark, rocky land. Here and there in the obsidian hillsides could be seen what resembled small caves, their entrances neatly formed by what appeared to be deliberately-shaped slabs of rock.

"What are those?" Rachel wanted to know.

"Chinese," said Braid. "That's where they live. Wherever gold is, that's where you'll find them. They're peaceable, mostly. When knives come out it's usually for something among themselves;

but when that does happen, it's smart to be elsewhere."

Rachel looked at him with her large, dark eyes, smiling, rubbing her gloved hands together, then leaned forward, stroking Half Moon's neck. "I've seen the miners' wagons in Coldheart," she said. "How do they get them into this place?"

"Down there," said Braid, pointing, "you can see a turn in the trail, the wheel-ruts. They go right on, following the river maybe three, four miles, so I've heard, then come up a stiff climb to where the shacks are."

Rachel gave what was almost a shudder. "A real bleak and ugly place, this. It reminds me too much of the wagon-camps. Come on, this is far enough. I'm cold."

He nodded. "Let's go home." They were now quite naturally and unsurprisingly a couple, and he now did not wish to recall what his life had been like before her, or contemplate any kind of life in the future in which she was no longer there. Bree had said to him: "*She's a real good girl, mister. You'll take care of her an' not strike her an' see to her churchin' when you can?*" Well, so far there had been no sign of any preacher, and Rachel herself seemed singularly unconcerned about that. He was aware, however, that was not necessarily the popular view in Coldheart, no matter what face individuals might choose to show him. *Braid's girl*.

"Come on!" she called, laughing, and clapped her heels in. He hauled the big black around and set out after her.

Later, walking on Main, shrugged down into his thick coat, Lowell, removing a cigar from his mouth, said to him: "Whatever the fine detail of it was, over there at Sands', it sure seemed to uncross a few eyes."

"In this job," said Braid, "you have to spend some of the time drawing lines an' the rest of the time persuading some people not to step across 'em;

but not so much that it gets bad for business."

"Now, I like the sound of that," said Lowell.

Braid nodded, walked on. A short while later he met Dalton who, choosing more elegant phrases than had Lowell, expressed sentiments that were in essence quite similar. Even Freda Moyle, a plump, rather prissy-mouthed woman he encountered coming out of a store, had a word or two, the first she had so far spoken to him.

"We are all relieved, very relieved, Mr Braid, that you've shown firmness on our behalf."

"I can only do my best, ma'am."

"I'm not sure what you've been told, Mr Braid. I don't go to town meetings. I leave that to my husband; but women in Coldheart have had to go about fearfully for too long. All kinds of low-life men have been wandering the streets, usually the worse for drink; and there have been regular brawls. And as you must know, lives have been lost.

Whatever happens outside Coldheart is not our concern. We simply wish to move around freely in our own town, day or night, in safety. As women, we have always had to be escorted the shortest distances, even to our own gatherings for Christian prayer."

Braid smiled slightly. "*In grief and fear to Thee, O Lord, We now for succour fly*."

Freda Moyle's plump hand fluttered to her throat. You've *heard* us?"

"Passing," said Braid, "in the night."

"It's a special hymn, did you know that, Mr Braid? It's so old; older than this whole country. It's a plea for protection from the plague."

"I didn't know, an' I've sure not got powers such as that," he said, "an' I doubt even Brooke has, but I'll do what I can with the other, ma'am." He raised his hat and moved away. Over all, when he came to think about it later, he felt that whatever matters he might have taken a hand in up until now, his worth was perhaps being measured most against his standing up to Hart. In places such as this, these things travelled quite quickly from mouth to mouth. In this instance, whatever was said would enhance and solidify the perception that was had of Braid.

Then something else occurred which in itself was sufficient to cause some in Coldheart to look at the marshal again, perhaps less favourably.

Wes Parrish came.

Braid saw him standing outside one of Coldheart's cafés, blowing inside one of his gloves, stamping his boots as though to restore circulation to his feet. As tall as Braid himself but of slightly thinner build, Parrish was dressed in levis tucked into the tops of black boots, a thick knee-length, dark-coloured coat and a shallow-crowned black hat, like Braid's own; and now his bony face was reddened with cold. He saw Braid about the same moment that Braid began to approach him.

"Braid! Well, by God you're a sight for sore ol' eyes!" They met, slapping shoulders, gripping hands, laughing. "Well . . . " said Parrish, poking a gloved finger at Braid's badge. "Well, well!" At the hitching rail stood a carefully-kept but right now well travelled roan horse with a good saddle on it, saddlebags, canteen and bedroll. Braid waved a hand towards it.

"From where to where, Wes?"

"From parts sou'-east to parts nor'-west. If up yonder's the high plain, what they call the Coldheart Plateau, I'm on my way across there an' down through the Flints to Carradine Forks. This route to it is high up an' it sure enough is cold, but the only other way I can figure out would be about a hundred miles longer."

Braid nodded slowly. He did not enquire what business might be taking this man to such an unlikely destination as Carradine Forks and thought that if Parrish wanted him to know he would eventually get around to telling him.

"You just got in?" Braid asked.

"Yeah, an' now I'm headin' right in here." He moved his head to indicate the cafe. Braid thought for a moment, considering whether or not to invite him for a meal, then for reasons he could not even begin to define, did not; but he did say, pointing:

"I'm down there. Before you push on, drop in. I'll find a bottle somewhere."

Later, Rachel said: "Wes Parrish? Who's Wes Parrish?"

"Sometimes, Rache," Braid said, "I wonder if I understand that myself, an' I've known Wes over twenty years, here an' there. For one thing, he's been a marshal in various places."

"A marshal?"

"Well, yeah. Sometimes. But the winds have always kind of blown Wes around. He's a real hard man, Rache. I could take you to some places that, on sight, would put a bullet in Wes Parrish. I could take you to some where there's men buried that he put there an' I'd not be prepared to say it was all in the course of duty or justice or whatever. A kind of this-way-an'-that-way man, Wes, an' damn' dangerous if he sets himself to be. I've seen him act generous to a fault, then so vicious you wouldn't want to know about it."

"I was about to ask why you didn't fetch him home for supper, but you changed my mind for me."

"Oh, you wouldn't have anything to fear from Wes; though once he got a look at you, I might."

"How long does he reckon to be here?"

Braid lifted his shoulders. "Passing through, he says, across the plateau, heading for Carradine Forks. I didn't ask him why an' he didn't say. If he'd told me, maybe I wouldn't have wanted to know. He might drop in the office for a drink." Then he added: "If his name gets around while he *is* here, somebody's bound to know it; or he'll be recognized."

Braid was right. After his meal Parrish had sought out a livery for the roan and a room for himself and had not long been in the Lucky Wheel for a drink or two before somebody nudged somebody else and muttered: "I seen that big bastard somewhere." Then: "By God, that there's Wes Parrish." Heads turned, some of them in slight alarm.

Over the next few hours it became freely known that Braid and Wes Parrish were on the best of terms, and that began to make people turn and stare at Braid himself after he had gone by, as though he might have become in some sense contaminated.

"Will this do you some harm?" asked Rachel with a shrewdness which belied her youthful looks. "Knowing this Wes Parrish?"

"Hard to say," said Braid. "But whether it does or not, I do know Wes, an' I've known him a long time an' been glad of it more than once, so that's that." He did add: "Whether or not I'd always trust him, though, that's another matter."

"I saw him today in the street. Well, from how you told me he looked, I'm sure it was him."

"And?"

"He made me feel . . . kind of scared. It was just a glimpse, passing, but his eyes, they seemed like two mirrors, just shiny, no depth; and no warmth."

When they had their drink in the office, Rachel was nowhere to be seen. Almost smiling to himself, Braid wondered if she was sitting down there in the kitchen with the carbine across her knees.

"So," said Braid, "you're set to move on."

Parrish sipped his drink, tongued his lips appreciatively, nodded, then grinned. "They've cottoned on to who I am, Braid, so they're prob'ly lookin' real hard at their marshal right now, wouldn't you say?"

"If any of 'em want the job," said Braid, "it's theirs."

Parrish's gaze roved around the

office, perhaps noting the empty gun-rack, lingered on the passageway leading to the cells and beyond. No doubt he would have heard about Rachel for he was nothing if not an inquisitive man, but in the event he did not say anything, and soon rose, extending a hand. "Well then, Braid, time's come."

Braid's were not the only eyes that followed the back of the tall man on the roan horse as he went riding slowly out of Coldheart, his collar turned up against the chill. One of Rachel's small, slim hands rubbed slowly up and down Braid's back as he stood in the doorway.

"He's gone?"

"He's gone," said Braid, not entirely certain what his feelings were, yet coming to the view that they might well be of relief.

During the late afternoon there were some snow flurries. The town itself had fallen quiet, most folk electing to remain indoors. In the saloons a few cowhands, heading away down out of this higher country, paid off, had tarried for some warming liquor. One of their number, a red-haired youth who chose to appear on the boardwalk in front of the Three Deuces to finish off a bottle, drinking directly from it, then discarding it by hurling it across Main, was thereupon disposed to relieve himself onto the street, even as Braid came out of a nearby store and instantly took exception, the upshot of which was the red-head's being taken along to the jail by Braid and put into one of the cells, there to contemplate his misdemeanours. "We can't have it," Braid told him. "You might easily have frightened Mrs Freda Moyle half to death." The youth looked at him in a glazed fashion, lay down on the bunk and went to sleep.

"Who is he?" asked Rachel.

"We might never know," said Braid. "If he wakes up an' starts carrying on, just try to ignore him. I'll throw him out after his hat in the morning. Right now I'll go down an' fetch his mount up to the barn."

When he had done that he wondered if it was even worthwhile making a tour of Coldheart, since more snow had been falling, the streets and the wet buildings now, in the early evening, a jumble of contrasts in black and white; but he did go out again.

Going by the freight office he raised a hand to the seemingly ever-working Ridley. Again, while pausing in shadows in a back-street, he saw Dalton, huddled and bent against the cold, slipping homeward. Had there been another figure, vanishing, parting from him? Braid thought so and was of the opinion that it might have been a woman. Perhaps the fears that Freda Moyle had claimed to be universal were less than was thought; but now the street was empty. He turned away, went trudging back onto Main. At the gunsmith's corner he glanced into the poorly-lit shop and saw Maria mopping the muddied floor. Braid was almost certain that when the girl looked up and saw him she was on the brink of motioning to him; but the door-curtain inside the shop was swept aside and Lutyens stood there jerking his long head sharply. Meekly, the girl, carrying her mop, went through to the room behind the shop. Braid walked on. He continued his patrol around the streets, breath vapouring, snow lightly drifting down; but after about a quarter of an hour, having taken a look out as far as the Cribs, he began heading for home along a street which paralleled Main, a way that was shrouded in a darkness relieved only randomly by lamps glowing from rear windows. There, for example, was the gunsmith's, the living quarters above the shop. A movement up there drew his attention. It was a second before he realized that what he was looking at was probably a bedroom window, for there was the girl, the naked back and shoulders of her, before a curtain was seized and drawn across, and it took another second or so for Braid to accept that what he had seen was the bony, deep-socketed face of Lutyens himself, with bare chest and torso, before the curtain had obscured them both. Braid went crunching onwards.

Rachel, pouring steaming coffee for him, asked: “What is it? What’s the trouble?”

He rested his head against the high back of the chair, holding bluish hands out towards the heat pulsing from the iron stove. “Oh, humanity, Rache.” They had just finished their coffee when they heard urgent footfalls out in the yard and a man’s hoarse call: “Marshal! Marshal! They’re at the Deuces, set fer a shoot!”

Braid came out of his chair, reaching for his damp coat and, struggling into it, said: “Bolt up after me.” All manner of things were running through his mind. It could be a highly dangerous situation that he was heading into. If drunken, unemployed cowboys were involved, it could be precisely the kind of mess in which, beyond rational thought, one of them might draw a pistol.

As she followed him to the door Rachel breathed "Take care," and even as he went jogging away he heard her slide the bolts home.

8

THE snow was no longer falling but even in the poor light, small, dirty drifts could be seen lined along the edges of the boardwalks all the way up Main. From down the street Braid saw that many of the buildings had lamps in them, among these the assay offices and, he thought, the bank and loan where there appeared to be some sort of activity. And here and there were wagons standing on the street and at least one drawn into an alley alongside one of the saloons. It was a scene that he had witnessed numerous times before, and he knew therefore that the wagons would be those belonging to the miners, perhaps numbering as many as a dozen in each and who would have come in with accumulated gold for valuation and safe deposit. That would also mean that any of the men whose business had been finished would now have gathered in the saloons. Fewer men from the range were appearing in Coldheart nowadays, however, and on this particular night there was no evidence of horses at the hitching rails. And whatever it was that was taking place in Ed Thomas' Three Deuces had not spilled out onto the street.

Braid went slopping across Main and onto the opposite boardwalk, passing men who gave him scarcely a glance, but as he reached the batwing doors of the saloon he undid his coat, letting it fall away to expose shellbelt and the dark reddish wood butt of the big pistol on his right thigh.

He went on in.

A large number of people were in the long, smoky room, men — mostly miners as he had expected — along with several of Thomas' saloon girls, these decked out in vividly-coloured costumes. There did seem to be some sort of argument in progress and Thomas himself in his light grey suit, ruffle-fronted white shirt and blue string tie, was on hand. Two miners were standing almost chest to chest, but whatever heavy dispute had been developing was quickly suspended when a bystander said something and Thomas and those arguing and eventually everybody else turned to see Braid coming down the room, people standing aside to allow him clear passage.

Thomas, beak-nosed, with small, searching eyes, nodded to Braid but gave no indication that he viewed him as a welcome sight. Thomas, Braid had discovered on short acquaintance, was a man who much preferred to be left alone, and was not disposed to accept advice. Thomas, despite Lowell's assumption during the first meeting with Braid, was not in particular a marshal's man, and right from the start he had always indicated as much, at least with his eyes. When Braid asked what the trouble was, Thomas said:

"It's not the sort of trouble we can't handle ourselves. Couple of these boys had a difference of opinion, but it's well on the way to bein' settled."

"Then nobody here sent for me?" queried Braid, an uncomfortable feeling beginning to overtake him.

Thomas at once shook his narrow head. "I thought you knew by now, Braid, in this place we like to kill our own Indians."

The unease Braid had begun to feel turned into a surge of annoyance.

"You've made that clear," he said, "but if they ever try to burn you down, just don't start yelling for a chain of buckets." Then pointedly dismissing Thomas he looked at the miners who had been at loggerheads but who had now fallen back a pace or two, both of them looking — how was it? — almost disinterested. "Do whatever you like in this dump, but take it out onto the street an' I'll throw the both of you in the cage to cool off, an' in these temperatures, that won't take long."

He turned and walked out of the saloon. *Disinterested.* There had in fact been something about the entire scene which had now begun to trouble Braid and it had begun even while Thomas had been speaking, something about the two who had been arguing and then, almost too willingly, stopped and backed off, something . . . what?

Main indeed looked dirty and bleak. *Something contrived.* He had been standing brooding about it, but now his leathery face came up. *Contrived.* As though it had all been a ploy. Then it seemed that something solid had struck him full in the belly. *Christ! Rachel!*

Braid leaped off the boardwalk and ran, slipping and sliding until he gained the filthy boards across the street. People who were abroad, huddled in coats, looked in some surprise to see the big man, the marshal, coat flung open, pounding along, splashing across alleys and sidestreets. One man from a saddlery even stepped out after Braid had gone by, to watch after him.

* * *

Rachel listened to the sounds of Braid departing, then went back to warm her hands at the stove. She never felt easy when he was called away, especially at night, and now that the sombre and bitter weather had closed over the town she sometimes felt miserable when she was left on her own. It was a face she took care not to show Braid.

When the sound came she went first to the door that led to the passageway to the cells and without opening it, listened, thinking that the boy who had been put into one of them had awoken and started moving around. So she was completely unprepared for the assault when it came. There was a single window in the kitchen over which she had seen fit to hang a bright curtain, which was now drawn, and with the sound of smashing glass this curtain was swept aside as someone outside, wielding a piece of wood, not only broke the window but could be heard clearing the jagged glass from the frame with it; then with frightening suddenness a man's head and shoulders came bursting in.

For a moment the girl was held fast, fear draining her limbs of strength, and by the time she was able to react, to take a step towards the corner where Braid had left the carbine, the man had fallen into the room among shards of glass; and before she had taken a second stride, there he was, bulking large, a solid man with a dirty skin and a large black moustache and dressed in brown cord pants, a thick woollen shirt, grey in colour with a black leather jerkin over it. He had no hat on and his black hair was falling over his face. She had never set eyes on this man before but there could be no doubting his intentions as he came up out of a crouch, grunting from all his efforts and started towards her, half growling, half laughing, saying something she could not quite understand, but which sounded like . . . *bastard's girl* . . . "

Rachel skipped backwards, seized the door handle and got herself through into the short passageway, hearing him in his heavy boots coming after her, then she flung herself through into the passage that ran beside the cells and arrived, scrabbling frantically at the door which opened into Braid's office. If she could just manage to get in there and cross to unbolt the outer door before this madman laid his hands on her, she could soon be out on Main, screaming, and even if Braid did not hear her, then surely to God someone else would, and come to help her. But the door to the office, though it was not bolted, was slightly distorted through dampness, and although she tugged at it desperately it would not open instantly; and even as it did, shuddering, one of the large hands of the man pursuing her was clamped onto one of her shoulders.

Braid fell when turning into the alley that led to the yard behind the jail-house, hurting his knees and the gloved heels of his hands, but the pain went almost unnoticed as he scrambled clumsily to his feet, bumping against the outer wall of the jail, then went pounding on in a sea of sludge and snow. As soon as he got into the yard he could see that the back door was still shut, but he was aware of sounds, voices, a scream from inside the place and a terrible fear gripped him. The glass had been swept from the kitchen window, the curtain had vanished, and on the ground outside, the snow had been churned up by somebody's boots; and near his feet was what looked like a pick-handle. Braid got his gloved hands onto the bottom of the window frame and with an immense effort born of a desperate fear for Rachel, heaved himself up, willing power into his arms until he lay with his midriff across the window frame, bruising his shoulders as he thrust his way inside, and then, like the man who had come in this way before him, fell into the room.

The kitchen was empty, the carbine

still propped in a corner, but banging noises were coming from the direction of the passageway leading up past the cells, so Braid went quickly through, lamplight from the kitchen at his back, his long shadow leaping ahead of him.

He was not prepared for what he now saw. In the passage was a man whom, even in this poor light, he recognized as the miner from the Cribs some while ago, Sholto. But Sholto's large head had been pulled hard back against the bars of the cell, and hooked around his throat was the bony arm of the red-headed cowhand that Braid had left sleeping in there earlier in the evening, and try as he might, heavy boots thumping against the opposite wall of the passage, Sholto could not do enough to break free. Beyond him, the street door of the office was now standing open, and limned faintly against outside light, was Rachel, out on the boardwalk.

"Rache!" She turned, came hurrying back in.

"Oh Braid, I'm real glad to see you."

To the cowhand, gasping from the effort of holding the big miner, pulled fast against the bars, Braid said: "You can let him go now son." When the boy did, and Sholto managed to stand away from the bars, his hands going to his own throat, his breath hoarse and rasping, Braid said to him: "You just made the worst mistake it's possible for a man to make." Braid hit him hard with a left hand punch, snapping his head back, then followed up fast, ripping left and right punches into Sholto's midriff, driving the breath from him; and when his upper body arched over, his head coming well down, Braid, seizing the thick hair bunched at the miner's collar, brought his right knee up with a solid yet curiously liquid thump into Sholto's unprotected face, hurling him up and backwards to pitch onto the floor of the office, knocking a chair over as he went down, Rachel having to move lithely out of the way, hands pressed to the sides of her face. Unhurriedly, Braid stepped over to Sholto and stooping, took hold of his leather jerkin and hauled him upwards; but Sholto, his face and moustache thick with rich, dark blood, could not stand, so when he was up as far as his knees Braid again brought his own knee up and with the sound of a melon struck with a hammer, Sholto was once more flung bodily backwards to the floor. But this time Braid was on him, straddling him, big fingers at his throat, bellowing he knew not what, in a paroxysm of fury, at first only faintly aware of Rachel's voice and of her hands pulling at his shoulders.

"No! Oh Braid . . . Braid . . . no!" Little by little the sound of her voice did come through to him and he became aware too, of her physical presence, and took his hands from Sholto's throat and sat back, though still straddling the prone, battered and bleeding miner. "He'd only just got to me," she said, "when that boy in there, in the cage, caught a-hold of him." Braid was breathing deeply. Sholto was alive but was barely conscious. Finally Braid nodded, and with Rachel clinging like a small girl to his arm, got to his feet.

"If he'd *touched* you, really *touched* you, I'd have killed him. Nothing could have saved him." He turned to the old desk and raked around in a drawer, then handed her keys on a steel ring. "Better let your rusty boy out."

She glanced at Sholto who was still down on the floor but beginning to make small movements. "What will you do with him?"

Braid stood massaging the knuckles of one hand. "What I should have done once before. He's on his way. He'll never get the chance to do this in Coldheart again."

Hesitating, she said: "You won't . . . do any more to him, will you?"

"No." Then: "This is the one that hurt Greta. Recall what I told you about places like this? The minute you think you've got control, that it's come to a time of peace, it'll jump right back at you."

She went with the keys and let the red-headed boy out and Braid heard them both going down to the kitchen and caught her voice, saying: ". . . Meal . . . "

When Sholto was at last able to stand, his face mashed and bloody, blood on his hands and his clothing, Braid said: "Do you own one of the claims?" Sholto nodded. Braid said: "You've got two options. You can sell and get right out of this territory, or you can stay up there, working it but never come into Coldheart again. I don't much care which one you choose but I can tell you this: show your face in Coldheart again an' I'll blow a hole in it." Sholto could not answer because he could utter no words through his ravaged mouth, but Braid was convinced that he understood.

When Braid had locked up and

returned to the kitchen the cowhand was seated at the table, a mug of steaming coffee before him, and Rachel was busying herself at the stove. The cowhand, now as sober as he would ever be in his life, was clearly in awe of Braid, accepting gratitude for what he had done in a kind of silent, down-headed confusion, while he himself seemed to cause in Rachel a pink but not unpleasant confusion by repeatedly addressing her as *ma'am*.

Supper over, having eaten it while watching Braid noisily boarding up the window, the boy now rose and prepared to depart, while Braid went to lead his pony out of the barn, saddled and with canteen, lariat and bedroll secured. Braid said: "Wherever you're headed now, it would be wise to stay clear of any miners still in town, an' certainly give the claims a wide berth."

When he had gone and they were back inside, Rachel warming herself, she suddenly turned and clung to

Braid. "Braid . . . Oh Braid, I didn't even have time to get to the carbine." For the first time since they had come to this place he thought that she was afraid; or perhaps it was that, for the first time, she was showing fear.

9

THERE was a poor, intolerant mood abroad. Rachel sensed it and decided it was not unlike that which sometimes overtook a family moving by wagon, and was chiefly because of chilling weather and the fact that people either could not, or felt disinclined, to move far afield.

"We're all wrapped up here in this place," she said, "on top of each other. All over, you hear people snapping, arguing."

"We don't," said Braid.

"Not yet," she replied, smiling in her wisdom.

They made certain that the horses got exercise and that they, themselves, therefore regularly rode out of Coldheart and even when, conscious of the fact that curtains twitched every time they went by, Rachel would return, swinging lightly down in the yard, her smooth cheeks flushed and her dark eyes sparkling. He could never resist watching the way she moved, for there was something fluid about her walking; and when she went quickly up and down stairs it was as though her small feet scarcely touched them, a light litheness, a body wafted hither and yon by some soft, fitful wind; and the touch of her long, pale fingers was like the touch of drifting feathers or of trailing silk.

Out of the blue: "I don't care what they think, Braid. They need you. Do you know what I heard?"

"No, what?"

"They call what they have here now, *Braid's peace*."

He gave her a wintry smile. He, too, had overheard it.

"They wouldn't have called it that last night if they'd seen me up at the Cribs, taking a shotgun off Cavvy Mitchel; or half an hour later, talking Mrs Cavvy out of slicing his throat with a saw-edged knife. She's more of a damn' handful than he is. An' the thing is, she wasn't bothered for one second that he might have blown my head off, only that he'd been up at the Cribs when it was all going on."

"I've seen some of them, the girls from up there. They look half starved."

"Just don't go giving 'em any more broth."

Braid's peace. If it was, it was a fragile thing. After what had been a couple of quiet nights a wild drunk drew a .36 Navy Colt and fired it at another man, rumoured to have been bedding the first man's wife, so that Braid had had to take the unusual and what he considered to be extreme step of drawing his own long pistol and disarming the demented drunk; and the very next night, a fight in the Blue Chip blundered and yelled its way into the street. To begin with there were three cowhands up against three or four miners, but one cowhand and one miner in particular stuck to it seriously and it was not until Braid arrived, swearing, and picked up a discarded wooden baton and sailed into the milling throng, that things began to settle down. But the lone cowboy and the miner, both fired up with drink, were by now down and rolling in the mud, still pummelling one another remorselessly. Braid moved in close, hitting first one, then the other with his baton, and when that produced no immediate result, began doing it again somewhat harder, and this time they went rolling apart, mud-covered, noses bloodied, and eventually, not without some difficulty, got to their feet.

Braid waved his arms, ordering everyone else away. Breathing deeply, hands on knees, the miner and the cowhand, heads hanging, breath clouding, were left in no doubt about their immediate destiny. Braid, showing them the baton, said: "Move ahead of me, that way." The cowhand, a ratty-eyed man in his middle twenties picked up his crumpled hat and would have stood his ground, but Braid shook his head. "Suit yourself. You can go with this other idiot up to that jail, or have this thing across your mouth. An' I wouldn't even consider trying to pull the weapon you've got there. Anyway, it doesn't look fit to draw." The cowhand, though more sober than he had been, nonetheless was none too steady on his feet, and with Braid looming over him, did not seek to push it any further; but he did say as they moved off, all three, Braid trailing:

"Yuh're beggin' for real trouble, mister."

Braid herded them along Main and in through the office to the cells, separating them once they got there. The miner at once complained that it was a damn' cold place and Braid thereupon assured him that it was intended to be. Their wet and muddied clothes were sticking to them and they had left a trail of filth through the office and passageway, getting to the cells.

Later, after locking up and walking

around and up the alley, Braid carefully left his own boots outside the yard door.

"There's two roosters up there in the cages," he told Rachel, "an' there's mud from here to there an' back again; but don't get in a fluster, they'll swamp out, the pair of 'em, before I throw 'em out in the morning."

"Do they need blankets?"

"Probably, but they're not getting any. They'd only foul 'em with mud."

"What about food?"

"No."

She stood with her hands on small hips, smiling slightly. "You're a hard man, Braid."

"It's all to do with this Braid's peace," he said.

Not long after that, the cowhand began shouting and when Braid became sick of it and went to see what he wanted, the man asked for blankets. Braid told him that if he continued making a racket, then he, Braid, would throw a pail of cold water over him, and from that point, life could only seem worse than it was now.

"You're makin' a big mistake," the cowhand said.

From the adjoining cell, squatting on the floor against a wall, arms crossed, hugging his own shoulders and speaking through puffed lips, the man said: "What he means, without sayin' it, is he's some kin o'that Hart bastard."

"Now I know where I've heard that mouth before," said Braid. "I should have picked it."

"We need blankets an' we need some chow," said Hart's kinsman loudly.

"For those things," said Braid, "you have to take care to keep out of the Coldheart jail. The Coldheart jail doesn't run to those things." He went tramping back to the living quarters.

"What did he want?" Rachel asked.

"Only things I don't supply."

"Did he want food, blankets?"

"Yeah."

Then, looking down: "I'm sorry."

"What for?"

"Questioning what you do. It's none of my business." He lifted her, swinging her up high and holding her. "Braid!"

"Always question me," he said, setting her down. "This time, it won't get blankets for those two an' it won't get any chow; but don't ever stop giving me the nudge when you think you should."

"You're a strange man." She took his hand. "Come on, it's past time we went up."

Next morning the miner and the kinsman of Hart, cold, stiff and miserable, did not want to swab the floor of the cells and the office, but Braid would by no means let them go until they had done it. They were, however, having very little to say now and while Braid was thankful for that, he knew that in all probability he had not seen the last of this cowhand, at least.

In the insipid, sunless light of day, a day overhung by gunmetal clouds promising further snowfalls, Coldheart lay with all its buildings made black by wetness, and under the eternal stench of unclearing smoke from its black chimney pipes.

Rachel went out wearing ruggy-looking clothes against the cold, for the purpose of visiting various shops along Main. One or two wagons bearing freight went by, cutting the mud, and about mid-morning, having, to judge from their soiled and miserable appearance, travelled some distance in bad weather, and heading for some equally distant though never specified destination, there appeared on Main a small detachment of the U.S. Cavalry comprising a pink-faced lieutenant, a resigned-looking middle-aged sergeant and eight troopers, one of these bearing a blue and white pennant on a long lance.

The troopers watered horses and stood around slapping their own arms and stamping their boots and followed with their eyes any woman who happened to pass by, while the officer undertook some negotiations in one of the cafés, these resulting in the entire detachment, apart from the lieutenant, going in for a meal; he walked up to one of the hotels, there to negotiate himself a hot tub with a solitary meal to follow.

Braid idly viewed this stiff-limbed military activity, then walked on to the far end of Main, and when he glanced up towards the Cribs, saw someone waving to him urgently. Boots crunching on frozen snow, he went to find out what they wanted and as he drew nearer he was astonished to see that it was Rachel.

"Rache, what are you doing up here?"

"I saw Greta," she said, "in the town. She'd been looking for Major Brooke but couldn't find him. Two of the girls are sick." Braid made no comment beyond asking:

"Where are they?" It was clear even to a layman that both of the women were running a high fever. Others had fetched extra blankets, and stoves had been stoked up, but the sick women, in adjoining shacks, were still shivering even as they were sweating. "Better that you go back now," said Braid to Rachel, though not unkindly, and to the anxious whores, said: "I'll go find the doctor. He has to be somewhere."

It proved to be not as easy as that. Up on the outside landing, Braid thumped repeatedly on the door and even tried the latch, to no avail. Wherever Brooke was, it did seem that he was not at home. Braid went carefully down the slippery steps, stood at the bottom, not knowing where to look next. He had discovered that Brooke was not particularly a drinking man, so did not frequent the Coldheart saloons, nor did he as far as Braid had observed, have many close friends here. A serious, solitary man, Major Brooke. Braid wandered along the boardwalk, rubbed at his cold face. Across the street, with a good deal of unnecessary shouting, the sergeant was getting his troop mounted, and he and it were thus deferentially assembled, in perfect readiness, by the time the boyish-looking lieutenant rejoined them and, mounting, called an impressive command accompanied by a gesture of white glove, and they all went slopping and jingling up Main, horses blowing and vapouring, the little pennant flicking in the cold wind.

Braid watched them until they passed out of sight. He did ask a couple of people passing if they had seen Major Brooke, but to no satisfaction. Once again he went back and climbed the dangerous steps and thumped on the door. This time, Brooke opened it.

"I called a little time ago," said Braid.

"I've been out," Brooke said. "Just got back." Braid thought that Brooke seemed warm and dry and certainly did not present the appearance of someone who had not long come in from the rawness of the day. When Braid then told him why he was there, expecting some sort of snappish resistance, Brooke surprised him by saying: "I'll fetch my bag. I'll go up there right away."

Back in his office Braid pondered over what people might have thought if they had noticed Rachel talking with the whore, then walking with her up to the Cribs; and he tossed around in his mind his belief that Brooke had indeed been in when Braid had called the first time, but had chosen not to come to the door. Braid stood up and went to his window to stare out across Main to the windows of Brooke's rooms above the assay office and soon came to the conclusion that from there, Brooke would have had a clear view of the place where the cavalry detachment had drawn rein. And Brooke's attitude had been unexpected. Without demur he had fetched his bag, and with his curious, stiff-legged walk, gone swinging along Main and beyond, up towards the Cribs, almost as though . . . as though *what*, thought Braid.

As though to *make up* for something? For what? For failing to answer Braid's first call? Braid shoved his hands in the waistband of his pants, thinking about Brooke.

His attention, however, was now drawn to a pair of riders who had just entered Coldheart, a sallow-faced man wearing an old slicker and a tall-crowned, dirty grey hat, the other bearded and wearing a long, moth-eaten coat of heavy material, brown in colour, and with a dark felt hat that looked as though it might once have belonged to a cavalry officer, but had had insignia removed, and by the general appearance of it, had been kicked around a few saloon floors since then. The recently-departed young lieutenant, Braid surmised, would not have been found dead in such a hat.

Braid was to sight these two again later as they emerged from a saloon and prepared to mount up, Braid easing back into a doorway, giving them careful scrutiny. Long ago he had developed an instinct about men such as these. They were something more than mere itinerants down on their luck. The horses they had were good, sound animals, the saddles the pair were now settling into had not come cheap. The riders carried no rifles but their movements had revealed long pistols in oiled, carefully-preserved holsters, these tied down. But it was their faces that Braid studied most intently. The sallow man, of average height and build, from his hairline to his neck on his left side, had curiously crinkled, wizened skin, as though at some time he might have been scalded; and his eyes were small and very still, jet black in colour, contrasting with the paleness of his face.

His companion, of heavier build and as tall as Braid himself, had greenish eyes and an unkempt black beard. He had a teak-hard face and it was a face that Braid thought he ought to know, but try as he might, he could put no name to it.

They had hung around in the town for an hour or two and from time to time Braid had made sure that he knew where they were. They made him feel uncomfortable. They were not ranch riders; they were definitely not miners. They were not simple drifters. They did not fit anywhere, and Braid did not like the looks of them at all. In fact he had made up his mind to approach them and had gone out to do so when he had seen that they were mounting up, their horses slewing and tossing, then moving at an easy, bobbing jog, out of Coldheart.

When he got home again, Rachel, looking up from food she was preparing, and who had also seen them, said: "Have they gone?"

He nodded. "Just rode out." He was pleased that they had gone and was just about to sit down when he straightened again quite abruptly. "By God, I know who he was. It was the beard; that an' time in between. When I saw him, years back, he had no beard."

"Who is he?"

"Dave Stemmer."

"Is he a real bad man, Braid?"

"Yeah. Oh yeah, he's a bad one right enough. Now, what in God's name would bring Dave Stemmer through a place like Coldheart an' in poor weather for travelling?"

"Maybe there's somebody after him. Anyway, at least he had the sense to keep going. Who was the other one?"

"I don't know. I've never set eyes on him before; but if he's with Stemmer, he's scum." Braid punched a fist into his other palm.

"What's the matter?"

"Oh, just Stemmer. I ought to have known him right off."

"Did he see you?"

"No. No. I don't believe he did, but he wouldn't have known me, anyway."

"Well, they've gone. Come on, wash up. The meals about ready."

They had gone, but for some reason Braid could not put aside the sombre recollection of them.

10

BRAID had got the feeling that matters had begun to pile up on him, what with Sholto and the saloon brawlers, and had also come by the impression that Rachel had remarked on, the generally quick-tempered attitude that seemed to be abroad. Indeed, with a wry look at him she had then commented to his departing back: "Don't go patting any dogs. I want you back here with both arms." He did in fact continue with his practice of patting familiar dogs but what he also did was to put the firm word out again to the saloons that they must try to contain their trouble more quickly and more positively; he also laid his eye on any group congregating near any of the saloons, and in such a searching way as to cause most of them, on his approach, simply to melt away.

Firmly but courteously he interviewed all newcomers to Coldheart, even those who, quite plainly, were merely passing through, and now he much regretted not having questioned Dave Stemmer and his companion when they had put in their brief appearance. Whenever some lone wagon came, even if only carrying a family on the move, Braid still posed a few casual questions; and when she thought he had gone, Rachel invariably came out bearing hot coffee and perhaps some home-made bread, produced with a larger stove with an oven that Braid had acquired for her; and she always watched such wagons out of sight, no matter how bad the weather. Perhaps, Braid thought, each single wagon was for Rachel but one wagon of memory, standing in a wet, cold camp by a scattered and dying fire, near a ford of the Finder River. Rachel, however, never spoke of it, though often, afterwards, there was an impression that she moved closer to him, at least for a time.

One night about now, another thing happened. He had encountered the undertaker, Lapin, and had had a short conversation with him, then not long after, went by the lighted window of the freight office and raised a hand to the ever-toiling Ridley. Ridley acknowledged him but, not for the first time in recent days, Braid formed the impression as Ridley looked down again at his paperwork, that he would not have welcomed Braid's actually coming inside the place; as though in some way Ridley might not now wish to encourage Braid's company, even to the extent of distancing himself. It was puzzling to Braid, but a short while later on that same night, he witnessed something by chance which perhaps offered another reason for Ridley's manner. Quite clearly this time he saw Dalton parting from a woman and he was close enough to them, though unseen himself, to recognise Alice Ridley.

"You think Mr Ridley *knows*?"

Rachel asked, her dark eyes widening.

"He's been acting different," said Braid. "He's not as forthcoming as he was to begin with. He used to have a whole lot to say for himself." Then: "I met Lapin, earlier. He passed an odd remark, asked if Dalton had said anything about another meeting."

"And has he?"

"Not to me."

"Will you ask him about it?"

"Maybe."

Braid continued to patrol the unappealing streets by night. Tonight, few but saloon lamps were still glowing. Once, turning, he thought he caught a sudden, stealthy movement, but when he went to look, found no-one. Later, in blackness, he came out of an alley onto Main and stood stock still at the sound of a single gunshot, loud in the night's stillness. It had not come from close-by, and a moment passed before he could estimate, confidently, that it had been somewhere in the general direction of the Cribs. "Christ!"

thought Braid. "Again." He set off along Main, trying to move at a jog but concentrating as much on keeping his feet in the slippery going. If the sound of the shot had prompted anyone in the town to come out to find out what was going on, he was unaware of it, simply keeping doggedly on, eyes probing the gloom ahead for any evidence of movement. What he had heard had definitely sounded like a heavy-calibre pistol, and one that had been discharged out in the open. Well, at least it seemed this was not to be a repeat performance by Cavvy Mitchell with his shotgun, on the wrong side of a bottle of bourbon.

As he drew nearer to the Cribs, Braid slowed his approach, seeing lamps shining in some of the windows but no obvious signs of activity anywhere outside. And there were no voices to be heard, certainly there was no screaming. He had just decided that he would make a circuit of all the shacks when, from out of nearby darkness a voice that he thought he ought to recognize said:

"Soon as the alarm goes up, who comes but the whoremaster."

Braid turned towards whoever it was that had spoken. There were, in fact, two of them. In the faintest of glows thrown by a lamp in the first shack, Greta's, he could now put a face to the man whose voice had seemed familiar; the cowhand who had claimed to be a kinsman of Hart's, and behind this man loomed Hart himself.

"Crenna was right," Hart said. "Attract his attention an' the sworn protector of whores would come a-runnin'."

They wasted no time in showing their intent, at once closing in on Braid, and Braid knew that up against two of them, Hart himself a tall, powerful man, he would have small hope of getting out of this without a severe beating or worse, so without preamble he launched an upswinging kick at the nearer one, Crenna, and had the satisfaction of landing his boot solidly, fetching a shriek of pain from Crenna and a wild flurry in the darkness. To Braid's advantage, the doubled-over and loudly-howling Crenna, holding his crotch, went blundering against Hart, coming in. As a breathing space, however, it was not to last long, and Braid and Hart, in poor footing, were soon slugging it out, Braid twisting to one side, anticipating an upcoming knee, and instantly he took advantage of Hart's brief uncertainty of balance to lash out and catch the man a blow which, however, skidded off a muscular shoulder on its way to clumping against Hart's head, and sent a pulse of shock up Braid's own left arm from a sharp pain in his fist. Braid was compelled to back off, flexing his gloved hand in pain, while Hart was on his hands and knees in slush, grunting, trying to gather his wits. Off to one side, barely discernible but certainly audible, Crenna was still down, still holding himself, and the sounds suggested that he was now vomiting. Hart then came up surprisingly fast, not punching but diving at Braid, catching him around the waist with an oncoming force that sent Braid staggering backwards, trying to seize hold of Hart but failing, both of them going down to roll over and over, in close; fists pumping, knees jerking up savagely, hoping to crotch the opponent. Hart, with a mighty effort, suddenly thrust very hard at Braid and shoved away from him and by the time Braid recovered, Hart was getting to his feet and then coming in again at Braid who felt a stab of agony in one shin before, in desperation, he managed to twist away from the onslaught. But the knifing pain in his left hand had intensified and he now knew that one of his fingers was broken, so from here on in he must fight the dangerous Hart virtually one-handed. Now though, as they circled one another, their eyes more accustomed to the gloom, and in the faint lamp-glow, Braid flicked the injured left hand out, taking care to whip the blow short of Hart who nonetheless instinctively withdrew his head, Braid swung a heavy right hand, catching Hart in the upper body, then, risking a slip, went quickly back just out of range of Hart's immediate reflex punch. Hart came charging in and Braid, unready, badly positioned for another right-hand blow, bent his knees slightly and shot out the left, but not with his fist closed, instead catching Hart's jaw with the heel of the hand, rocking Hart's head up, then moving his right foot across fast, Braid, thrusting his right shoulder across in front of Hart, slashed the right fist around in a fierce reverse arc, not a punch but a chop, catching Hart across the exposed throat, sending him backwards in arm-splaying disarray, gasping and choking. In cold anger now Braid went with him, grasping with his right hand the back of Hart's head and, even as he had done to Sholto, smashing a knee into Hart's face as it came down.

Hart lifted explosively, seemed to hang a moment, then slumped down. Braid came swiftly to him again. Faintly, so that Braid almost missed hearing it, Hart said: "No!" Undecided, Braid hesitated, his left hand paining him badly now, his own face and body afire with other aches from this man's brutal punches. Chest heaving, gasping for breath, Braid said:

"Never let there be another time between you an' me. If there is, I'll do what maybe I should've done here an' now. I'll cripple you."

Somewhere in the nearby dark, Crenna was still moaning and spitting. Braid moved painfully around until he found his own hat which had come off during the fight, picked it up and went none-too-steadily away towards Coldheart.

* * *

He was in the tub, his splinted left middle finger held up clear of the steaming water, and Rachel, her apron damp, was busily soaping his back.

"Don't move around, the water's slopping over. Oh my . . . Braid, you're bruised all over. What did he have, a pick-handle?"

"Not that I noticed," said Braid. "Anyway, his damn' hands were worse than any pick-handle."

"How could they *do* this?"

"Pride," said Braid. "Men like Hart don't like being made to look second-best. Throwing one of his kinsmen in the cage was only the excuse to set it off."

"I'll never understand them," she said, "men like them." Then: "Major Brooke was kind of strange. When I went to fetch him, he looked . . . *embarrassed*."

"He's not a man who's easy to work out." He gave a gasp when she poured water over him to rinse the suds away.

"And when he was here, he spoke to *you*; only to *you*. He didn't even want to look at me. Stand up now. *Carefully*. I'll dry you. Then I'll use the salve that Major Brooke left. Oh, Braid . . . these *bruises*! Is it worth it?"

"Hart an' Crenna didn't offer me a choice. But I'd say that that's it. Hart's had his try, the one he was spoiling for. It'll be a while before Coldheart sees him again."

"So now there might really be a Braid's peace here?"

"That's what I think right now. But I've been wrong before."

"Oh, and with all this going on, I forgot; Mr Dalton was here."

"Dalton? When?"

"Not long before you got home. It must've been while you were still up at the Cribs. He knocked at the back door and called out who it was but I made him go around to the boardwalk outside the office and I lit the lamp so I could see it *was* him. He looked . . . flustered. He wanted to talk with you, of course. There's to be a meeting, an hour before noon, at the bank."

Stiffly, Braid was now pawing around with clean clothes. "That must've been what Lapin was on about. A meeting. Did he say what about?"

"No, and I didn't ask. He sure didn't want to look at me though. Like Major Brooke didn't either."

"I can't help it if they're both fools. They don't know what they're missing."

"Maybe they're going to pay you more money."

"An' maybe the sun will shine on Coldheart any minute."

"Never mind dressing," she said. "Get yourself up to bed. Your other clothes will have to be dried and brushed off. I'll do that before I come up."

Getting up the stairs was a more painful experience than he had anticipated and even when the subtle softness of the bed seemed ready to envelop him warmly and soothingly, he did not readily drift into sleep;

thus he was still on the outer edge of consciousness when he felt her slipping in beside him and was aware of the silkiness of her small body beginning to move over him.

11

SNOWCLOUDS still dominated Coldheart and a few flakes were spiralling down. Braid was now very sore and his joints were stiff; various abrasions were still stingingly apparent despite Rachel's gentle ministrations with Brooke's salve; and the splinted finger on his left hand was proving most awkward. He did go out early to try to free up his limbs but soon became depressed by the unappealing sight of the town, where little else was moving, and walked back to the jail office where Rachel, as though using some kind of mind communication, appeared with scalding coffee and bread rolls, and with his good hand he squeezed her around her slim shoulders until she squealed for him to stop.

During the course of the morning,

though activity continued to be subdued, the news did filter through that, contrary to popular and alarmist predictions, no dangerous infection of a nature more virulent than a debilitating influenza was raging among those up at the Cribs, and therefore Coldheart was not, as had been feared, under some unimaginable threat; an important reassurance, Braid thought, especially to the likes of Mrs Moyle and all her night singers: "*O shield us lest we die*."

He went trudging up to the bank for the pre-noon meeting, his damaged hand eased carefully into a pocket of his short, fleece-lined coat, his collar turned up, Braid feeling none too content, angry, still, with Hart and his kinsman, angry with himself at being so effortlessly gulled by them. He had lowered his guard, gone rushing in and had paid a price for it, a price that might well have been heavier. He could have lost his life. His breath went vapouring before him as he walked along, the sky above him leaden, Coldheart starkly black and white wherever he looked, the penetrating smell of the ever-present chimney smoke clutching at his throat. An obsequious little clerk with thick eyeglasses and a shiny, hairless head, showed him where Mr Dalton had said Mr Braid was to go when he arrived. The clerk's expression suggested that in all his life he had never seen at close quarters anybody quite as big and as mean-looking, and right now as obviously ill-used, as the man who came tramping at his heels.

There were six of them already in the room, though notably absent was Lowell from the Lucky Wheel and the women who had been at the first meeting. They had provided a chair for Braid. Dalton was there of course, presiding, on his own ground, Ridley it seemed, this time taking a back seat; Moyle was there, plump, round-eyed and a mite uncomfortable, Braid considered. Lapin, narrow-faced and with his customary headcold was on hand; Brooke, his stiff leg stuck out, was there also, fussily patting his pockets but apparently not finding whatever he was seeking; and to Braid's — to say the least — surprise, so too was the sour Lutyens.

The room had no heating so Braid, like most of the others, did not take off his coat, but in order to sit comfortably he had to work his bad hand out of the pocket, and as soon as he did so, the splinted finger drew all their eyes except, of course, those of Major Brooke whose handiwork it had been. Presently, when they tired of looking at Braid's broken finger and taking note of his badly cut and bruised face, they looked to Dalton to open proceedings.

The banker cleared his throat, glanced at Braid, then down, then at Braid again.

"We have to begin by saying that there is, er, a great deal of satisfaction here in Coldheart at the way matters have been handled since you took on the job of town marshal."

"Matters," Braid said, as though interested in the word.

"The way . . . the way you have, ah, *taken hold* here," said Dalton acting like a man who had got ready to say quite a lot but was now having a hard time getting started on it; and nobody else appeared anxious to offer him any help. Finally it was Braid himself who said:

"I've got my own ways of dealing with . . . matters. Some people accept my way of going about things, others don't. Last night I was duped by a couple of men who didn't accept them an' they badly wanted to make that point."

Now Ridley stirred in his chair and did say something.

"I hear that it was Hart an' his cousin or whatever he is, that man Crenna. Nobody will have much sympathy for either of 'em an' if it means they'll now stay clear of Coldheart, I say so much the better."

There was a low murmuring that Braid took to mean assent. He was not entirely surprised, for he had found that there were people in Coldheart who did go in actual fear of Hart. Yet he could not help wondering what Lowell or Sands or Ed Thomas might think about what Ridley had just said, since groups of other men tended to go where Hart went, all hard drinkers and dedicated gamblers. Right now it might not be seen as overly important since the cattle outfits had long since paid off riders, but it might be seen differently in the spring when the ranches began hiring again.

"People are saying," said Lapin, "that we've had the most peaceful time that Coldheart can remember. Sure, there's been trouble but not a patch on what we used to have, an' a lot more things that might've turned sour, didn't, because you've *been* there, Braid, on the streets, day an' night. I say, in the finish, that's what counts, the town's law bein' *seen*."

Braid nodded slowly. Now that they had got the discussion moving they had tended to look less uncomfortable and perhaps less aware of the cold. Even Moyle and Lutyens had been nodding and murmuring agreement. Only Major Brooke, occasionally twitching irritably in his chair, seemed somewhat impatient as though, Braid thought, they had not yet come to the real reason for this meeting and he, for one, was a man who had other, perhaps more pressing, things to attend to. In fact, after a brief hiatus it was Brooke, his bright little eyes moving from face to face, who said: "Suppose we get to the point?"

Dalton shifted in his seat. "Yes, well, to be frank Braid, it's not so much about what's been happening on the streets that we wanted to talk about, but about the, er, what they call the Cribs."

"As I understand it," Braid said, glancing at Ridley, "they're not reckoned to be part of the town."

"True," said Dalton. "True." There was a round of nodding.

"So what about them?"

"This is what about them," Ridley said. "We'd like to see 'em closed down, have those women moved on from here."

"If they're not part of the town," said Braid blandly, "I don't see how the town can decide that."

"They still have an *effect* on this town," said Ridley. Brooke said in his crackly voice:

"It's not simply a matter of what they *are*, as far as I am concerned it's partly a question of public health. Right now there's an outbreak of influenza; next week or the week after it could well be something worse than that, something more dangerous that could well sweep through this entire community."

"Only if the town has close contact, surely?" said Braid mildly, looking not at Brooke but at the chubby, shifty Moyle. Moyle, for his part, peered worriedly at Braid, who made sure that a glance that was loaded with meaning passed between them; and Moyle slowly sat back in his chair almost as though attempting to retreat from Braid and indeed from the whole discussion.

"Some contact," said Brooke sharply, "is inevitable; some is unavoidable. You yourself have called me in not once but twice over matters connected with those shacks; the second occasion," he added maliciously, "coming about through one of the women venturing into the town and approaching someone for help." They all looked as though they were well aware who he was referring to, though he did not mention Rachel by name.

"Help which you'll admit was needed," Braid said steadily.

Lutyens, in an oddly hollow-sounding voice, suddenly spoke up. "Any kind of disease could be brought here like Major Brooke says. It ain't usual for this town to encour — to have them women comin' here."

"They've always needed to buy food," said Braid, "an' to my knowledge, nobody's refused their money. There are times when they'll need a doctor. They needed one yesterday."

"And they got him," snapped Brooke. "They got him." He shifted his stiff leg slightly as though to emphasize what he had said. "But as I see it, they're not entitled to call on Coldheart law, which is paid for by the town. That's a different matter entirely."

"I'd best make something quite clear," said Braid then. "I'm not of a mind to leave any woman screaming no matter who she might be an' no matter where she might be. A town line — somebody's notion — drawn on the ground won't ever change that for me; an' if a shot's fired at night, anywhere *near* this town, I consider that to be my business too, an' will in the future." He took time to look at each of them in turn, then said slowly, now looking only at Lutyens: "If a man came here who had a grudge against you, Lutyens, an' fetched a rifle with him, he might see fit to stand well off, maybe on that higher ground west of Coldheart an' try to pick you off from there. He might wait, say 'til after nightfall, take a shot through your back window, upstairs. Now, whether he hit you or not, or maybe by mistake, hit your daughter, I'd feel bound to go on out an' find him an' deal with him. More than that, I'd be expected to. So this town can't have it an' not have it."

Lutyens' deeply-set eyes fastened on Braid, then closed for what seemed a long time before they opened again. Braid had calmly passed the message that he had set out to pass. Lutyens' long face, naturally pale, had now drained of what little colour was there and the man himself seemed to shrink where he sat; yet no-one else in the room appeared to have noticed anything at all unusual. It was Dalton who drew Braid's attention away from Lutyens.

"Even so," he said, unwilling to let it go, "even if we do concede something of what you say, having exerted a . . . a community *will* in this town by bringing back the law, there's a strong feeling here that now we ought to go one step further and see to it that the, er, unsavoury place just north of us is finally done away with. Not only are those women up there not wanted because of *what* they are, but by being there, they attract other vermin from all over."

Braid's eyes sought Moyle but the plump trader managed to get himself almost concealed behind the larger shape of Ridley and was in any case staring at the floor.

"I've moved around Coldheart a hell of a lot, especially at night," said Braid then. "There's hardly a corner of it I haven't been into, one time or another." (Lutyens was now looking fixedly at his own boots.) "You wanted your streets made safer, day an' night, an' as it stands," he said, looking squarely now at Dalton, "your women can move from place to place, even at night, an' even if, sometimes, they have to go some way alone. Why not be satisfied with that? If there's any trouble up around the Cribs it can be taken care of the way it has been up to now." And to Brooke: "If the women up there were examined at regular times, like they do in some places I've been to, there'd be less chance of disease." When he glanced again at Dalton he could see at once that a change had come over the banker's face and when Braid then looked deliberately towards Ridley, and back to Dalton, he knew that he had sent his next message and that it had been completely understood by the quick-witted Dalton. As Brooke again opened his mouth to say something it was Braid who got in first. "Major Brooke, here, should be able to verify what I'm telling you. The army well knows how to deal with this kind of thing Major?"

Brooke's face flushed and his glance stabbed at Braid but he nodded jerkily.

"From time to time," he said, "the army has had to take such situations in hand."

Braid said, pinning Brooke with his eyes: "As a matter of fact there was a detachment through Coldheart only yesterday. Pity you were missing at the time, Major, you could've made yourself known to the officer. He was a boy who might not have known what those Cribs were, but I'd lay any odds his old sergeant did."

Brooke now regarded Braid with unfeigned dislike but, with an effort, kept his mouth shut. Braid, for his part, did not know, would maybe never know, what particular nerve he had struck within this choleric surgeon, only that without doubt, he had struck one. Of those at the meeting only Ridley and Lapin now seemed interested in keeping it going.

"What we wanted to say," said Ridley, "is that by closin' those Cribs, cleaning 'em out an' not allowing the likes of 'em to come back, we'd give some of the worst element no excuse to come near Coldheart."

"What he says is true," Lapin put in. "Some of our own women here believe it's a long way past time that a . . . a moral stand was taken." Both he and Ridley looked pointedly at Braid himself. So here it was, and it had taken a good long while for them to get around to it. *Some of the women*. Not one woman was here, yet in fact all were here, with Mrs Moyle and all her band of songbirds, having sent these men to say all that they had been saying and primed with words like *moral stand*; and underlying what Lapin had just come out with was disapproval of Braid and how he lived. No, more of Rachel, for that was always the unfair way that it was done. They would stop short of saying it in plain words, just as, all along, the Coldheart women had held back from saying it outright to Rachel. "*Nothing said. Just the way some of them look.*"

The problem here, however, as far as Ridley and Lapin were concerned, was that they had not realized that theirs were now the only voices besides Braid's now being heard at this meeting and would perhaps never come to see that, for some unknown reason the others, one by one, had become less positive, subdued into an uneasy silence.

Braid thought that he had heard about enough, and the intense cold in the room was almost another physical presence.

"Well," Braid said, "I have to tell you this." They all stared at him. "There's nothing that you or anybody else can say that will make me go up there to the Cribs an' turn the women out. What I might think about them being there doesn't come into it." As Ridley looked as though he might break in, Braid held up his good hand. "You've had your say, now let me have mine. So if it's left to me, I'll never close the Cribs. For one thing, if

I had to do that I'd have to close all the saloons, an' you've already heard my views about that. I'd have to close 'em because the girls there, Lowell's an' Harve Sands' an Thomas' girls, all use the top rooms for the same purpose as other girls use the Cribs, except the whores at the Cribs make no pretence about it, an' the saloons get their cut. I won't try to shut the saloons so I won't touch the Cribs. Now, it's been made plain here today that what I've just said to you is right against what you an' other people in Coldheart want, the same people, some of 'em that pay me to keep the peace an' take their instructions. I make it a rule never to stand against them that pay me; so that has to bring me to the last thing." Awkwardly, with one hand, he unpinned the worn old badge from his coat, and standing up somewhat stiffly, walked across and dropped it on Dalton's desk. "We'll be on our way, both of us, in a couple of days." They were too taken aback to respond immediately and before they were able to recover, he was at the door, but paused before leaving. "By the way, her name is Rachel; Rachel Olvie. You can tell your women that it's not a name set to explode in anybody's mouth if they've a mind to say it out loud." He closed the door behind him.

* * *

With swift insight, Rachel said: "Was it really all because of *me*, Braid?"

"No, because of *them*; the kind of people *they* are."

"Do you think that they'll try to have you change your mind?"

"There's some might think about it; but a few I could name will reckon it a damn' sight more comfortable to see the back of me, an' as soon as possible." He glanced at her keenly. "But you, you never even got a chance to say what you wanted to do."

Her long black lashes came down, then she looked up again. "I don't care as long as you still want me with you." A little later, she said: "Why didn't you say what you thought of them, Braid? It's not like you to hold back."

Braid grinned icily. "Sooner or later," he said, "because they're *who* they are, things will come to a head, will come out. It's only a matter of time." He gave her a quick light tap on the tip of her small nose. "Just think, we can sit here, you an' I, an' look into Coldheart's future."

She giggled. "You're a terrible man, Braid." Then: "Where will we go?"

"I hadn't thought very far ahead."

She said: "Braid, do you suppose there's any place called Warmheart?"

"We'll never know unless we go an' look," said Braid.

12

THE black horse moved solidly against him and he stood back. He was in the barn, having made a careful check on both the animals, taking time over the condition and firmness of shoes. Now he went tramping inside and along to the front once just in time to see Rachel departing, going out early on this very cold morning to buy herself new boots for the impending journey, new levis and a long slicker. She promised she would return quite soon, when she would sort out all of the possessions that were to be taken with them. When Braid warned that while he had every intention of purchasing a pack-horse, he had no plans to buy a wagon as well, she poked her tongue out and went flitting away before he could say anything else.

Braid stripped, cleaned and oiled the long pistol and then the carbine and he had loaded the pistol and had just finished feeding in cartridges through the side-slot to fully load the tube magazine of the carbine, when Rachel came back through the front door with all her goods, her cheeks aglow but seeming somewhat less ebullient than she had been earlier. Braid looked at her keenly, all his senses prickling.

"Trouble?"

She nudged the door shut with her foot, then crossed and dumped her parcels on the old, scratched desk alongside the weaponry. "I'm not sure. Braid, when that man you know, that Wes Parrish was here, I got only a kind of glimpse of him. I kept out of the way; but just now, I thought I saw him."

"Wes? Back in Coldheart? Where?"

"Look, I'm not real sure it *was* him; but *if* it was, there were two other men with him and one of them looked like Stemmer."

"*What?*"

"Stemmer."

"Yeah, I heard what you said, Rache. Where?" He got up out of his creaking chair and went across to the door and opened it, admitting another chilling lick of outside air. He stood squinting up and down Main.

"They were up near the general. I wasn't all that close to them."

Certainly, he could see some horses that had been hitched, along that way, but there was no sign anywhere of their riders. Finally he came back in, closing the door behind him. "Wes Parrish, Dave Stemmer an' one other. Whoever the other one is doesn't much matter. If Parrish is here with Dave Stemmer, that's not good news Rache, not good at all."

"Whether it's good or whether it's bad is no longer your affair. Now, you don't have to answer for anything that happens in Coldheart. If they've come here to burn it down, which might not be such a bad idea at that, it's not your concern. You left the badge with Mr Dalton; let *him* pin it on. Braid?"

He seemed hardly to have heard her and was already lifting the heavy shellbelt, holster and long pistol, passing the belt around his body, buckling it, bending, tieing the holster down.

"I sure do know that, Rache." And as her mouth opened again: "Listen . . . listen to me a minute. If Parrish *is* with Dave Stemmer, maybe something is on the go in Coldheart." Still holding a hand up for her to wait for him to finish: "Don't you see? Stemmer an' whoever this other rooster is might not have known I was here or even who I was, but Wes sure did. When he was through Coldheart I was the law here. So if there is anything going on, what do you think the first thing Wes would think of doing?"

Fingers went to her lips and her dark eyes widened.

"Oh Braid . . . Braid, I hadn't thought . . . " She moved to him and he enfolded her, but only briefly. He stood away and reached for the carbine. "I'll go take a look."

"The carbine. Why? Your hand . . . "

He held up his splintered finger. "I know; but Wes had no rifle that I saw, when he was here, an' I didn't see one on Stemmer's horse or the other feller's. If anything does happen, this thing could make all the difference." She helped him on with his thick coat. A waxboard box still lay on the desk, open. He picked out a handful of faintly greasy cartridges with one hand and pushed them into the right-side coat pocket and, wordlessly, Rachel put further rounds into the left pocket; and it was she who fastened the coat for him just as a sleet-shower struck at the window. "Shit!" said Braid. Then: "As soon as I'm out, bolt this door, then go down right away, an' bolt the back one, an' don't forget the one in the annexe." He reached his hat down off a peg, put it on. "If you *do* hear any shooting, for God's sake don't come out. Stay in here, wait for me."

"Braid . . . Braid, take real good care. Don't . . . start anything."

"If anything starts it won't be me that does it."

The sleet-shower had spent its first fury. Braid, going out, had a last glimpse of her small face, heard the bolts slide across behind him.

The sleet had become rain. Braid stood on the boardwalk, the carbine held down alongside his right leg, looking up along a miserable Main. The hitched horses that had been outside the general store had gone from there but he thought he could see them — if indeed they were the same ones — further up the street and on the opposite side. A wagon with a four-horse team was coming ponderously out onto Main from about where Ridley's place was, but nothing else was stirring. "*I'm the only damn' fool out in the rain*," thought Braid. Yet if it was them, somewhere in Coldheart, what would bring them back, all three together? The bank would. It had come instantly to his mind when Rachel had come in the door, saying: '. . . *there were two other men with him and one of them looked like Stemmer.*'

Braid worked his shoulders inside his coat, water dripping freely from his hat. He might just take a walk along there and have a look, run his eye over the place, maybe even call in to see Dalton on some pretext. He paused. Someone had come out of a building about halfway along the street, on Braid's side, a man, one who stopped briefly under a porch, blowing on his hands, glancing up at the leaden, moving sky, rubbing his hands, then thrusting them down in the pockets of what looked like a thigh-length grey coat, then began to come along with a rather shambling walk in Braid's direction, tending to hunch over in the wet. Braid shifted his eyes to the hitched horses way further up on the opposite side of Main, thinking that, momentarily he had seen other movement there.

He was not sure, for the distance was misting with rain. His attention came back to the man walking towards him, crossing the muddly outlet of an alley now, then along the boards again; yes, a thigh-length coat, cord pants maybe, a tall-crowned hat. Braid stared. Well, whoever he was, he was not Wes Parrish nor, indeed, was he Dave Stemmer; he was not big enough. This man was within maybe eighty feet of Braid, one hand still in a pocket of the coat, looking at where he was putting his feet, with an awkward gait on high-heeled boots, clinking with spurs still attached to them. *A tall-crowned hat*. It seemed to be a dirty grey in colour. Stemmer first came to Braid's mind, but only as one of two mounted men, the other wearing at that time an old slicker and a tall-crowned hat. At sixty feet Braid half turned towards him and felt sure there had been a momentary checking of stride. If it was the man who had been with Stemmer, what might

Parrish have said to him? "*Yuh can't miss him, Braid. Big bastard with one o' them fleece-lined coats — yuh can see the fleece at the collar, an' he'll have an old badge on the coat.*" If so, the tally would now have come up short, for there was no badge to be seen. Maybe then, in the very next instant, maybe the oncoming man saw the carbine against Braid's right leg as Braid had turned slightly, for he stopped abruptly right outside a saddlery, under its verandah; Sturton's place it was.

Braid dropped to one knee fast for he saw the right hand coming up out of the coat pocket, the glint of the long pistol emerging with it; and none too soon, for as the pistol came clear the man blasted a shot away and lead fanned Braid as it passed just above him, and even as Braid fetched the carbine up, resting it on his damaged hand and let go a thundering shot that flung splinters from a verandah post, the gunman had got himself into

Sturton's doorway and then into the shop itself.

Braid levered a new round in as he went forward. When he got nearer to the saddlery he could hear a man's voice, Sturton's perhaps, shouting something, and when he got as far as the window there indeed was Sturton, his mouth hanging open and an expression of shock on his old face. When Braid filled the doorway Sturton waved one of his mottled hands towards the rear of the premises. "On through . . . He run on through!" As far as Sturton was concerned, whoever the man with the drawn gun had been he had obviously been intent on getting out of somebody's way in a hurry after sudden gunshots, and now here was Braid, looking like Sturton had never seen him look before.

Braid did not go on through the shop but went out and headed towards the alley that he had watched the man cross, earlier, and with rain still pattering on him, went splashing into the muddy by-way and broke into a jog. The farther end of this alley gave onto a back street running parallel to Main.

Almost as soon as he got there he saw the man, though he had got a good start on Braid, for Braid had not been able to move as quickly along the slippery alley as he would have wished, a price he had had to pay for not wanting to blunder into the man somewhere in the back of the saddlery. Two things were conflicting now in Braid's mind; stopping this unknown man who had tried to shoot him, and trying to find out where Parrish and Stemmer had got to. The man in the thigh-length coat was in no mood to check his stride long enough to take another shot at Braid, clearly wanting to get himself out of range of the carbine that he now knew Braid had. Braid's breathing was burning from his efforts, he was wet, water masking his face and blurring his vision. So he stopped, went to one knee, bringing the butt-plate of the carbine to his shoulder, his left thumb and forefinger forming a V under the tubular magazine that ran below the 22–inch barrel. As he fired, rain swept across his line of sight, the carbine bucking, acrid smoke dispersing quickly. The running man had not gone down but Braid believed that he had hit him, thumped him sideways, but when, impatiently, he dashed more water from his eyes, there was no longer any man to see.

Braid rose, levered a new round into the chamber and went trotting forward, making for the last place he had seen the target, water leaping away from under his boots as he went. There was a barn, an empty corral and a lumber yard. Braid paused, looking at the stacks of wet lumber gleaming dully in the rain; and before it vanished in a rain-pool, saw a fresh boot-mark, and nearby a spatter of watery pinkness. Man-spoor. In his boyhood, Braid had been cautioned about following any wounded wild animal into brush where, hurt, but alive and silently enraged, it might be lying in wait. Nonetheless, he went on. Just then, borne on the wind he heard the sound of a gunshot, muffled, but in the direction of Main. Instinct told him to go at once to find out what was happening; necessity urged him to seek out a quarry already hit.

He found him near the end of a lumber-stack; or first, he found the long pistol, an old weapon but well-kept, droplets gathered individually on the slightly oily surface of the metal. The man lay on his face, arms flung out, just as he had fallen, blood running from him being immediately diluted in the rain-pools. Propping the carbine in his left hand, Braid leaned down, legs straddling the man, and with his right hand turned him over, flopping him heavily onto his back like something waterlogged. The bullet had gone in under the right armpit and presumably was still in him, and it was a wonder to Braid that he had got this far before he went down and indeed had still carried the pistol in his right hand almost all of the way. No doubt of it, this was Stemmer's companion, sallow and with that large scar that looked like a scald. Braid straightened, walked away.

After that one distant and somewhat enclosed-sounding gunshot he had heard no more but Braid, cursing the rain, slipping and sliding, ran on as best he could through it, angling towards a street that would take him close to the corner where the bank stood.

Once there, he could see a few faces in doorways that had a view of the bank, all staring in that direction, and sure enough there were three hitched horses outside the bank, but otherwise no signs of activity. Rain was still persisting, washing away some of the small snowdrifts and everything in sight was dripping or cascading with water. Braid now considered what options he had. In poor footing, he could cross the muddy street, and once he reached the boardwalk opposite, go inside, head-on and take his chances on what happened next, not knowing where Parrish and Stemmer would happen to be at the time, and thereby put at risk all who were in there with them, Dalton, the three or four clerks he had noticed when he had been in the bank, and perhaps some townsmen; or he could try to work his way around the building and attempt to get in another way, hoping that he would be neither seen nor heard while he was about it. That seemed to be far the better plan; but there was one other thing that he could do first, and he now set out to do it.

Getting across to the bank in falling rain, through thick mud, would have been problem enough at the best of times; doing so across this open space where three streets joined, with the threat of Parrish or Stemmer emerging while he was stranded part-way and exposed, was palpably more dangerous; but he kept determinedly on, the mud sucking at his boots at every sluggish step, and finally gained the boardwalk on the opposite side. As quickly as he could, Braid moved along the heads of the horses, unhitching each of them. One backed off, head coming up. Braid took off his hat and though he made no sound, waved it wildly, water spraying from it, and all three horses threw up their heads, blowing and whickering, backing away. One walked as far as the middle of the street and stood looking at Braid; the other two wandered another ten yards and stopped, backs towards the slant of the rain, the breath of all three clouding out, and all far enough now from the boardwalk to make getting out to mount any of them no simple task.

Braid, bending low in an effort not to show himself at windows, now went urgently along one side of the building to a single window in one of the back rooms, trying a nearby door but discovering, as he had expected, that it was securely bolted. He cupped a hand at the wet glass and saw what could have been the same spartan room in which the townsmen's meeting had been held. The inner door was closed and the room was empty but for one remaining chair. He tried to raise the window but it refused to budge. Noise or no noise he could afford to lose no more time; he must get inside the place. Nearby lay an empty wooden crate, the bank and loan's name stencilled on it. Braid tipped it over, placed it below the window and climbed up on it; then, as Sholto had done outside his own kitchen, though using the curved iron butt-plate of the carbine, bashed the glass in, and again using the butt, swept flush the glass along the bottom and the sides of the frame. Within a few seconds he was up and over and onto the floor inside the room, listening intently. Beyond the sound of the rain on the roof he could hear nothing, though that did not necessarily mean that the sound of breaking glass had not been heard elsewhere.

Through the inner door he passed

into a short passageway and went along it as quietly as he could, the recollection of where he now was relative to the main room of the bank, coming back to him.

They were still in there. As Braid eased closer to a partly-open door, the whole scene lay before him. The big room had counters made of dark wood and edged with brass strips, and brass grilles, and in behind the counters several wooden desks and chairs and a number of wooden file-cabinets, and behind the row of desks, an open space and then a strong-room, the door to which was now standing open. The room was lit by the yellowish, wet-day glow of several hanging lamps, each with a green metal shade. In one corner a pot-bellied stove glowed, its round, narrow chimney-stack standing through the roof.

Dalton was there, coatless, under the threat of a pistol held by a man in a long brown coat, Stemmer, stuffing banknotes into small canvas sacks, Stemmer wagging the long barrel impatiently. Wes Parrish, less concerned with haste, was standing alongside one of the clerks who was transferring small pieces of gold from metal boxes into soft leather wallets with drawstrings attached. Beyond, someone was lying on the floor and two or three others kneeling over him, attending him in some way.

Braid withdrew slowly. If he were to go in there now, the way the people were placed, any shots that were fired could well hit some of the bank's people, and indeed it did seem that one of them had been shot already. If it developed into a real bad shoot, then by this time tomorrow, Coldheart could be trying to dig half a dozen holes in very wet conditions. He could now hear a heavy, husky voice, Stemmer's, saying: "Come on! Come on fer Chrissake!" One thing was in Braid's favour; either there had been no townsmen in the bank when it was hit, or if there had been they had somehow got out. For what seemed like an age, Braid waited until, under the rain-sound, he heard Parrish's hard, calm voice saying: "That's it. Let's be goin'." And presumably to Dalton and the others: "Get on the floor an' stay there." There came the sound of boots pounding and when Braid eased into the long room, Wes Parrish, several of the small canvas sacks strung together, in his left hand, his slicker gleaming, was heading on through the street door, Dave Stemmer with his own sacks at his heels. As Braid appeared, Stemmer glanced back, at once astonished to see the big man, armed and coming in, and roared: "Jesus! Carbine!" and boomed a too-hurried flash of a shot behind him, the slug clanging, setting one of the metal lampshades swinging wildly, lights and shadows leaping, Stemmer almost climbing over Parrish in his efforts to get out, a bluish swirl of gunsmoke going out with them both.

Calling "Keep down!" to those prone behind the counter, white faces, wide eyes turned towards him, Braid vaulted the counter and went charging down the room, realizing at once that in going over he had again hurt his left hand.

Outside, Parrish and Stemmer, upon seeing that the horses had been turned loose, reacted differently, Parrish, cool enough to buy time, immediately heading around the corner of the bank looking for cover or for opportunity. Stemmer, however, having been badly shaken by the knowledge that a man whom he assumed to be Braid was somewhere behind him and carrying a carbine, failed to weigh his options and went off the boardwalk, slopping out through the mud towards the nearest of the horses.

Braid stood in the bank doorway, not yet out in the rain, and shouted for Stemmer to stop; but Stemmer went lurching on towards the horse, which as he reached for it, threw its head up, whickering, and went backing away from him. In desperation Stemmer turned, and making odd weaving motions of his upper body, his bearded face dripping, his eyes bulging, brought his pistol-arm up. Braid, propped now in the doorway, calmly shot him, the carbine bucking, a waft of acrid smoke washing around Braid, and Stemmer, hit solidly high on his left side, had his body clouted around, the pistol flying from him as though he had thrown it away. Leaving his canvas sacks where they had fallen, his hands and knees deep in the ooze of the street, Stemmer began trying to crawl away, his dark felt, cavalry-looking hat gone, his bearded face drooping, the long brown moth-eaten coat trailing.

Braid levered another cartridge in and shot him again, and this time Stemmer's big head was punched savagely sideways, pinkish spray bursting from it, and at that point his crawling was all done and he lay partly on his left side, partly on his back, bleeding profusely, the rain cleansing him, to go on bleeding and be cleansed over and over. Braid levered yet another cartridge in and set off to find where Parrish had got to. His attention went beyond, then returned to a livery further down on the opposite side of the street. Braid was about to move along the boardwalk, aware of increasing pain in his left middle finger, pain spreading up his arm, and looking, saw that the splint was broken, when another thought struck him. Going this way as he was, afoot, he could well lose Parrish, carbine or no carbine. He turned and ran back the way he had come and at the bank corner leaped right off the boardwalk as Stemmer had done, sliding and splashing his way out towards one of the loose horses, but not choosing the one that had backed away from Stemmer. It seemed a long while before he could grab hold of a saddle, gasping, his face rivered with rain, and dragging one boot out of the mud and then the other, crawl himself up and finally swing one leg over and get into the saddle.

Reins wound around his throbbing

left arm he clapped booted heels into the horse's sides and got it moving in the direction of the livery, this as he saw Parrish, mounted on a saddled horse, make his appearance. Even from that distance he could see Parrish's teeth flash in a smile and one gloved hand half raised, as Parrish then headed his mount away out of Coldheart, out beyond the mining company building towards the Cribs, Braid urging his own horse in pursuit. Braid called out but his words were plucked away in the rain. As Braid himself left Coldheart behind and came abreast of the Cribs, Parrish turned in the saddle and there was a flash and a waft of smoke, but it was a wild one, a bad miss.

Braid eased the horse down and finally stopped. Even in the rain with the horse tossing its head and screwing sideways, he raised the carbine, tracked the riding man and squeezed his shot away. Sure that he had seen Parrish's body jerk, Braid again set out after him. Within the next half minute he knew that he was closing the distance between them for the horse up ahead seemed to be slowing noticeably and finally he saw it come down to a trot and then a walk and soon it stopped; and as it did so Parrish fell heavily off it.

When Braid drew nearer, Parrish's horse was standing a little distance away, the canvas sacks still slung across it. Parrish himself had now got up into a kind of crouch. There was no sign of a wound on him, but he had got one all right, for his face was drained of colour and though he was still holding the big pistol he seemed to be acting as though it had grown inordinately heavy.

When Braid drew his horse to a halt, twenty feet separated him from Parrish, and Parrish, his breathing ragged and rattling, said:

"Knew I couldn't rely on that bastard Slavin but Dave spoke up real good for him."

"Not like you to mix with amateurs, Wes."

"Always . . . a first time. Anyway, you're allowed one . . . bloody mistake."

"Not in this game," said Braid.

Parrish almost laughed, but not quite, and he tried his utmost to raise the pistol high enough to fire it, but failed to do that, also; but Braid shot him anyway.

By the time Braid came riding back into Coldheart leading the horse with Wes Parrish's body slung over it, his left hand was paining him very badly indeed, and several people, some of whom he knew, had begun congregating around the bank door, while a couple were at Stemmer's body. When Braid saw Dalton there in the doorway in his shirtsleeves, and Brooke just pushing his way through, Braid said: "There's one in a lumber yard as well." And jerking his head. "This is the last of 'em." Then: "I had to cross the Goddamn town line to fetch the bastard."

He left them, riding slowly away along the street in the rain.

13

MAJOR BROOKE had been the previous night and Braid's newly-splinted finger was again comfortable, and today he had helped Rachel pack their belongings into much more capacious saddlebags, bought from Sturton. The horse he had mounted outside the bank — which turned out to have belonged to Parrish — Braid had taken over to be used as a pack animal.

While he had been with them Brooke had not wanted to hold a conversation, though somewhat surprisingly he had acknowledged Rachel with a nod; but he had said, when Braid had asked him, that the bank clerk (who, it appeared, had tried to run and had been shot down by Stemmer) might survive, though Brooke had said it was too early to be certain.

Now it was mid-morning as Braid, Rachel and the well-loaded pack-horse came out of the alley next to the jail in cold but clearing conditions, Braid dressed as he usually was in levis and his thick coat and shallow-crowned black hat, Rachel in her new boots and levis, the short coat similar to Braid's and — a last-minute acquisition — a hat also resembling his, but pearl-grey in colour. But even in all this masculine apparel, her gentle, feminine movements were enough to give her away, and at close quarters it was impossible not to be struck by the soft delicacy of her features.

They rode along side by side, the end of the long leather lead from the pack-horse wound around Braid's saddle horn.

"Well," she said presently, "nobody came."

"No."

"Doesn't that make you angry? It does me."

"No, I'm past anger."

"I don't understand any of it, Braid. And that Parrish. In he came, smiling. He drank with you. Then he sent some man — a man you didn't even know and who didn't know you — to *kill* you."

"I told you before, it's not easy to understand men like Wes. This is a damn' hard an' unforgiving country, Rache. It makes some men, like Wes, into what they finally are. Wes himself couldn't have explained it to you, either. Don't waste your time trying to fathom him, it won't get you anywhere." In a little while he glanced over his shoulder. They were now somewhat higher than the town which was lying under its familiar haze of chimney smoke; black, mostly, was Coldheart, black with wetness, its streets brown ribbons of mud; an ingrown community, Braid thought, hesitant and fearful, always peering out from behind dark, grimy windows.

"What will they do now, do you think, about the law?"

He shrugged. "I don't know. Maybe they'll find somebody. They found me. If not, maybe they'll just have to sing louder."

Somewhere, sometime, maybe more than a hundred years on, someone might come upon a very old photograph, one taken by a practitioner just passing through, attempting to record — capture for posterity he might have said — a glimpse of those far-off times in such places as Coldheart; a group of townspeople obviously dressed against the weather, persuaded to pause for a few minutes outside what seemed to be a freighter's, some men, some women, different shapes and sizes, and not one of them smiling for the camera. And to one side of this group, the fuzzy images of two other people, these sitting on horses, a big man and a much smaller person, probably a girl wearing a mannish jacket and an odd-looking hat with a round, basiny sort of crown and a wide brim. Anyone caring to examine this photograph in detail might well be left with the impression that these two, whoever they were, were not meant to be there.

The horses clipping shoes over flinty rock, leather creaking, Braid cast one last glance behind him before Coldheart passed from his sight, then turned again to face the way they were heading.

Rachel had not even looked back.

THE END

Other titles in the Linford Western Library:

TOP HAND
Wade Everett

The Broken T was big. But no ranch is big enough to let a man hide from himself.

GUN WOLVES OF LOBO BASIN
Lee Floren

The Feud was a blood debt. When Smoke Talbot found the outlaws who gunned down his folks he aimed to nail their hide to the barn door.

SHOTGUN SHARKEY
Marshall Grover

The westbound coach carrying the indomitable Larry and Stretch headed for a shooting showdown.

FIGHTING RAMROD
Charles N. Heckelmann

Most men would have cut their losses, but Frazer counted the bullets in his guns and said he'd soak the range in blood before he'd give up another inch of what was his.

LONE GUN
Eric Allen

Smoke Blackbird had been away too long. The Lequires had seized the Blackbird farm, forcing the Indians and settlers off, and no one seemed willing to fight! He had to fight alone.

THE THIRD RIDER
Barry Cord

Mel Rawlins wasn't going to let anything stand in his way. His father was murdered, his two brothers gone. Now Mel rode for vengeance.

ARIZONA DRIFTERS
W. C. Tuttle

When drifting Dutton and Lonnie Steelman decide to become partners they find that they have a common enemy in the formidable Thurston brothers.

TOMBSTONE
Matt Braun

Wells Fargo paid Luke Starbuck to outgun the silver-thieving stagecoach gang at Tombstone. Before long Luke can see the only thing bearing fruit in this eldorado will be the gallows tree.

HIGH BORDER RIDERS
Lee Floren

Buckshot McKee and Tortilla Joe cut the trail of a border tough who was running Mexican beef into Texas. They stopped the smuggler in his tracks.

BRETT RANDALL, GAMBLER
E. B. Mann

Larry Day had the choice of running away from the law or of assuming a dead man's place. No matter what he decided he was bound to end up dead.

THE GUNSHARP
William R. Cox

The Eggerleys weren't very smart. They trained their sights on Will Carney and Arizona's biggest blood bath began.

THE DEPUTY OF SAN RIANO
Lawrence A. Keating and Al. P. Nelson

When a man fell dead from his horse, Ed Grant was spotted riding away from the scene. The deputy sheriff rode out after him and came up against everything from gunfire to dynamite.

FARGO: MASSACRE RIVER
John Benteen

The ambushers up ahead had now blocked the road. Fargo's convoy was a jumble, a perfect target for the insurgents' weapons!

SUNDANCE: DEATH IN THE LAVA
John Benteen

The Modoc's captured the wagon train and its cargo of gold. But now the halfbreed they called Sundance was going after it . . .

HARSH RECKONING
Phil Ketchum

Five years of keeping himself alive in a brutal prison had made Brand tough and careless about who he gunned down . . .

FARGO: PANAMA GOLD
John Benteen

With foreign money behind him, Buckner was going to destroy the Panama Canal before it could be completed. Fargo's job was to stop Buckner.

FARGO: THE SHARPSHOOTERS
John Benteen

The Canfield clan, thirty strong were raising hell in Texas. Fargo was tough enough to hold his own against the whole clan.

PISTOL LAW
Paul Evan Lehman

Lance Jones came back to Mustang for just one thing — revenge! Revenge on the people who had him thrown in jail.

HELL RIDERS
Steve Mensing

Wade Walker's kid brother, Duane, was locked up in the Silver City jail facing a rope at dawn. Wade was a ruthless outlaw, but he was smart, and he had vowed to have his brother out of jail before morning!

DESERT OF THE DAMNED
Nelson Nye

The law was after him for the murder of a marshal — a murder he didn't commit. Breen was after him for revenge — and Breen wouldn't stop at anything . . . blackmail, a frameup . . . or murder.

DAY OF THE COMANCHEROS
Steven C. Lawrence

Their very name struck terror into men's hearts — the Comancheros, a savage army of cutthroats who swept across Texas, leaving behind a bloodstained trail of robbery and murder.

SUNDANCE: SILENT ENEMY
John Benteen

A lone crazed Cheyenne was on a personal war path. They needed to pit one man against one crazed Indian. That man was Sundance.

LASSITER
Jack Slade

Lassiter wasn't the kind of man to listen to reason. Cross him once and he'll hold a grudge for years to come — if he let you live that long.

LAST STAGE TO GOMORRAH
Barry Cord

Jeff Carter, tough ex-riverboat gambler, now had himself a horse ranch that kept him free from gunfights and card games. Until Sturvesant of Wells Fargo showed up.

McALLISTER ON THE COMANCHE CROSSING
Matt Chisholm

The Comanche, McAllister owes them a life — and the trail is soaked with the blood of the men who had tried to outrun them before.

QUICK-TRIGGER COUNTRY
Clem Colt

Turkey Red hooked up with Curly Bill Graham's outlaw crew. But wholesale murder was out of Turk's line, so when range war flared he bucked the whole border gang alone . . .

CAMPAIGNING
Jim Miller

Ambushed on the Santa Fe trail, Sean Callahan is saved by two Indian strangers. But there'll be more lead and arrows flying before the band join Kit Carson against the Comanches.

GUNSLINGER'S RANGE
Jackson Cole

Three escaped convicts are out for revenge. They won't rest until they put a bullet through the head of the dirty snake who locked them behind bars.

RUSTLER'S TRAIL
Lee Floren

Jim Carlin knew he would have to stand up and fight because he had staked his claim right in the middle of Big Ike Outland's best grass.

THE TRUTH ABOUT SNAKE RIDGE
Marshall Grover

The troubleshooters came to San Cristobal to help the needy. For Larry and Stretch the turmoil began with a brawl and then an ambush.

WOLF DOG RANGE
Lee Floren

Will Ardery would stop at nothing, unless something stopped him first — like a bullet from Pete Manly's gun.

DEVIL'S DINERO
Marshall Grover

Plagued by remorse, a rich old reprobate hired the Texas Trouble-shooters to deliver a fortune in greenbacks to each of his victims.

GUNS OF FURY
Ernest Haycox

Dane Starr, alias Dan Smith, wanted to close the door on his past and hang up his guns, but people wouldn't let him.

DONOVAN
Elmer Kelton

Donovan was supposed to be dead. Uncle Joe Vickers had fired off both barrels of a shotgun into the vicious outlaw's face as he was escaping from jail. Now Uncle Joe had been shot — in just the same way.

CODE OF THE GUN
Gordon D. Shirreffs

MacLean came riding home, with saddle tramp written all over him, but sewn in his shirt-lining was an Arizona Ranger's star.

GAMBLER'S GUN LUCK
Brett Austen

Gamblers seldom live long. Parker was a hell of a gambler. It was his life — or his death . . .

ORPHAN'S PREFERRED
Jim Miller

Sean Callahan answers the call of the Pony Express and fights Indians and outlaws to get the mail through.

DAY OF THE BUZZARD
T. V. Olsen

All Val Penmark cared about was getting the men who killed his wife.

THE MANHUNTER
Gordon D. Shirreffs

Lee Kershaw knew that every Rurale in the territory was on the lookout for him. But the offer of $5,000 in gold to find five small pieces of leather was too good to turn down.

RIFLES ON THE RANGE
Lee Floren

Doc Mike and the farmer stood there alone between Smith and Watson. There was this moment of stillness, and then the roar would start. And somebody would die . . .

HARTIGAN
Marshall Grover

Hartigan had come to Cornerstone to die. He chose the time and the place, and Main Street became a battlefield.

SUNDANCE: OVERKILL
John Benteen

When a wealthy banker's daughter was kidnapped by the Cheyenne, he offered Sundance $10,000 to rescue the girl.

RIDE A LONE TRAIL
Gordon D. Shirreffs

The valley was about to explode into open range war. All it needed was the fuse and Ken Macklin was it.

HARD MAN WITH A GUN
Charles N. Heckelmann

After Bob Keegan lost the girl he loved and the ranch he had sweated blood to build, he had nothing left but his guts and his guns but he figured that was enough.

SUNDANCE: IRON MEN
Peter McCurtin

Sundance, assigned to save the railroad from a murder spree, soon came to realise that he'd have to fight fire with fire, bullets with bullets and death with death!